The Bed Mate

Also From Kendall Ryan

The Bed Mate

A Room Mate Novella

By Kendall Ryan

1001 Dark Nights

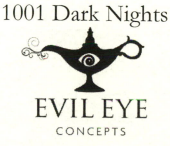

EVIL EYE
CONCEPTS

The Bed Mate
A Room Mate Novella
By Kendall Ryan

1001 Dark Nights

Copyright 2017 Kendall Ryan
ISBN: 978-1-945920-52-3

Foreword: Copyright 2014 M. J. Rose

Published by Evil Eye Concepts, Incorporated

Acknowledgments from the Author

I would like to thank my dedicated team for helping this book come to life, each in your own way. A big thank-you and a tackle-hug to these fabulous ladies: Liz Berry and MJ Rose, Danielle Sanchez, Alyssa Garcia, and Lauren Blakely.

An immense amount of gratitude goes to my readers. I love writing about all the bumps in the road on the way to a happily-ever-after, and I'm so thankful that you love reading about them. Let's never break up, okay?

I would like to thank my family for standing by my side and supporting my dreams, no matter how "out there" they might have seemed. Of those, my husband is my biggest and best supporter, and my rock. He believes wholeheartedly that I can do anything I set my mind to. I know I don't deserve his never-ending love and devotion, but I'm so thankful for it.

Sign up for the 1001 Dark Nights Newsletter
and be entered to win a Tiffany Key necklace.

There's a contest every month!

Go to www.1001DarkNights.com to subscribe.

As a bonus, all subscribers will receive a free
1001 Dark Nights story
The First Night
by Lexi Blake & M.J. Rose

One Thousand and One Dark Nights

Once upon a time, in the future…

*I was a student fascinated with stories and learning.
I studied philosophy, poetry, history, the occult, and
the art and science of love and magic. I had a vast
library at my father's home and collected thousands
of volumes of fantastic tales.*

*I learned all about ancient races and bygone
times. About myths and legends and dreams of all
people through the millennium. And the more I read
the stronger my imagination grew until I discovered
that I was able to travel into the stories... to actually
become part of them.*

*I wish I could say that I listened to my teacher
and respected my gift, as I ought to have. If I had, I
would not be telling you this tale now.
But I was foolhardy and confused, showing off
with bravery.*

*One afternoon, curious about the myth of the
Arabian Nights, I traveled back to ancient Persia to
see for myself if it was true that every day Shahryar
(Persian: شهریار, "king") married a new virgin, and then
sent yesterday's wife to be beheaded. It was written
and I had read, that by the time he met Scheherazade,
the vizier's daughter, he'd killed one thousand
women.*

*Something went wrong with my efforts. I arrived
in the midst of the story and somehow exchanged
places with Scheherazade – a phenomena that had
never occurred before and that still to this day, I
cannot explain.*

*Now I am trapped in that ancient past. I have
taken on Scheherazade's life and the only way I can
protect myself and stay alive is to do what she did to
protect herself and stay alive.*

*Every night the King calls for me and listens as I spin tales.
And when the evening ends and dawn breaks, I stop at a
point that leaves him breathless and yearning for more.
And so the King spares my life for one more day, so that
he might hear the rest of my dark tale.*

*As soon as I finish a story... I begin a new
one... like the one that you, dear reader, have before
you now.*

Chapter One

Maggie

"Fifth bar of the night!" Jeremy's speech was slurred but his eyes were filled with an unholy glee.

"Personal best," Peter agreed with a snort, holding up a hand for a high five that Jeremy attempted to oblige him with but failed, swinging wildly and almost toppling off his chair.

Excellent.

I rolled my eyes and sipped my vodka soda, glancing out of the corner of my eye to see Sam's expression. He wasn't drunk like his other two friends—he was too responsible to let himself get trashed in public. Either way, though, I knew at least two of them were only sips away from tearfully telling me how much our collective friendship meant to them, and I so did not want to stick around for that.

"Maybe we ought to hit the road," I murmured to Sam, jerking a thumb over my shoulder toward our drunken companions. "These two can grab a ride, right?"

"Wait, wait, wait." Jeremy held up a hand and then dropped it back in his lap with a smack. "We didn't get to the main event."

"Yeah," Peter agreed, clicking his beer against Jeremy's.

"Maybe we better talk about it another night," Sam said

with a patient smile.

I shook my head and sighed. *This ought to be good.* "What's the main event?"

Sam rolled his eyes. "It's what my genius friends have taken to calling our big snowboarding trip."

"Not exactly." Jeremy eyed Sam, then turned to me. "The main event for tonight was going to be us convincing you to go. Peter and I figured if we got enough booze in you, you might reconsider."

I swirled my drink with its tiny red straw and frowned. "And how do you think your plan is going so far?"

"You tell me." Jeremy waggled his eyebrows comically. "Don't you want to spend more time with us on the snow-topped mountains of Colorado?"

"Appealing as that sounds, no," I shot back with a grin.

"Come on. You have no idea how it feels to slice through the powder on your snowboard," Peter protested. "It's like heaven on earth."

"I also have no idea what it feels like to break my leg, but I don't want to find that out either," I countered easily, taking another long pull from my drink. "Did you know that more than forty people died snowboarding last year alone? A snowboarder who gets on a mountain twenty times a year is likely to be injured once every seven years. You can't argue statistics like that."

"It *could* be fun…" Sam hedged with a shrug.

"Breaking my femur after wildly careening down the side of a mountain? I think not."

Sam gave me a dead-eyed stare. "Not that part, scaredy cat. The trip, I mean. These guys aren't right about much but you should come along. We're doing New Year's in style. Hot tubs and hot toddies in a winter wonderland."

"Did you not get the stats I sent you the last time you tried to convince me to go snowboarding?" I demanded.

"Some of us don't live our whole lives by the numbers," Sam said, a teasing light making his dark blue eyes sparkle.

Stop it, idiot.

Best friends weren't supposed to notice things like that about each other. It was just weird.

"I fail to see what's wrong with it." I shrugged, feeling suddenly warm despite the relative chilliness of the room, and sucked down the rest of my drink.

"Come on, Mags. Take a risk." Those eyes searched mine and, despite myself, I could sense my resolve weakening. I hated saying no to him, even when his daredevil lifestyle threatened my cocoon of safety. We were as different as night and day, but for some reason, we clicked and I felt more comfortable around him than pretty much anyone else.

A stab of guilt shot through me and I cleared my throat.

"I really can't. Trevor and I probably have plans, I just can't remember what they are." I pulled out that feeble old excuse and Sam glanced at his other friends before turning his attention back to me.

"Right. Trevor. Hey, you need another drink? Or a water?" He pointed at my empty glass.

"Nah," I said. "I'm ready to crash for the night if you think Heckle and Jeckle will be okay without us here to babysit." I jerked my head toward Peter and Jeremy, and Sam laughed.

"Come on, guys, let's head out. I'll give you a ride." He snagged his coat off the back of his chair and slung it over my shoulders before motioning for his friends to join us as we moved to the bar to settle up.

"I've got hers and mine," he said to the bored-looking bartender. I protested, holding my hand out, but he moved away before I had the chance to argue.

"You don't have to do that," I said.

"I think I can handle a vodka soda on my bill." Sam's lips twitched into the confident grin that had always made all the girls swoon.

The other guys paid their tabs and collected their cards and, together, we all made our way to Sam's massive truck. Still snapping insults back and forth, the two boys hopped in the back of the extended cab while I took my spot up front and rolled down the window to feel the crisp, winter air.

"It's going to snow," I said.

"It better. If I don't take my nephews sledding soon, they're going to murder me," Jeremy murmured.

I nodded. "You're in luck, then. I can sense it coming."

I breathed in deep. Maybe winter sports weren't my thing, but there was nothing I liked better than the smell on the air just before the snow. It reminded me of Christmas or a cozy evening by a crackling fire with a book in one hand and mug of hot cocoa in the other. All the things that made wintertime on the east coast the best time of year.

"You're going to catch your death with the window down like that," Sam warned.

"Ha! Look who's the conservative one now?" I crossed my arms over my chest triumphantly. "Seriously, though, you know how I love the smell. Just let me leave it down for one more minute," I pleaded.

He laughed and nodded like I knew he would.

We made our way to Jeremy and Peter's apartment first and, after making sure they had their phones, wallets, and keys, dropped them off. Silently, we watched them make their way to the front door as the first flurries of snow drifted to the ground. When they'd disappeared behind the wide metal doors of their complex, I turned to Sam again.

"Never again without a warning," I said flatly.

"With them?" He chuckled. "I know. I actually didn't know they were coming for sure until last minute or I would've warned you. They were in rare form tonight."

I laughed. "That's one way to put it. I've never seen Jeremy give his number to so many women in one night."

"I've never seen the women get rid of it as fast, either. Just balled up bar napkins piled high like fallen soldiers." He tsked in mock sympathy.

"If he cooled it with the cheesy lines, he would probably do better," I said, rolling up the window with a sigh.

"I heard him tell that redhead by the jukebox that she looked like his first wife."

"Ouch," I said with a laugh and then paused. "Wait…he's never been married, has he?"

Sam shot a wry grin in my direction. "Exactly."

I covered my eyes with my arm and groaned. "Ugh. Jeremy, why?"

For the next few minutes on the ride to my place, we deconstructed the rest of the night, chatting comfortably.

As we turned on to my street, dread began to close over me like a dark cloud until I remembered Trevor wouldn't be waiting for me. He'd asked to stay over tonight and I'd begged off. The sense of relief washing over me didn't bode well for my current relationship, and I vowed that tomorrow, I'd finally do what I'd been putting off for months.

The old tried and true pros and cons list.

That settled, I was feeling slightly less like garbage as Sam pulled up to the curb in front of my apartment building.

"I'm not tired. Want to come in and watch bad Christmas movies with me?"

"Christmas is over."

"Never too early to start for next year," I argued. This, too, was something Sam knew. My Christmas movie collection was extensive and full of favorites.

I tended to break out my collection mid-October, easing into the season with *The Nightmare Before Christmas*, but by this time of year and straight through January?

It was a new movie every night. I had a lot of ground to

cover.

"Besides, I have something for you," I added, sweetening the pot in case my promise of an awful movie hadn't convinced him.

"You broke our rule again, didn't you?" Sam asked.

I grinned. "You're going to like your present."

"I always like my present, but you're not supposed to get me one. We had a deal. And, again, quick reminder… Christmas is over."

"Exactly. So I didn't break the rules. It's an early birthday gift. And you're going to really like it. Like, really, really like it."

"Fine, then you can give it to me in February for my birthday." His firm mouth quirked into a crooked half-smile as he surveyed the road in front of him and I knew I had him. "And understand that, when you get me presents, it really sets the bar pretty high for what I'm going to get you in return."

"I don't know what you mean," I said, pulling the huge shoulders of the borrowed coat around me.

"Yes, you do," he said, shooting me an incredulous stare. "You're a super-human gift giver. Nobody can compare."

I swung open my door as he turned off the ignition and we both hopped out of the car.

"Super-human is a bit of a stretch," I said as and we stepped out into the gently falling snow and made our way to the double doors.

"It's not," he argued, holding the door open for me and then stepping through. "Like that gift from last year—"

"I just pay attention is all." I shrugged.

"But who else would get someone the exact replica of their train collection from childhood? You contacted my mother behind my back for pictures," he reminded me as we climbed into the waiting elevator.

I pressed the button for the third floor and frowned. "Your gifts are thoughtful, too. I love my body wash collection. I now have a fragrance for every mood."

This was true. For every birthday, holiday, or special occasion over the past eight years, Sam had gotten me a different kind of soap and lotion gift basket. At first I wondered if he thought I stunk, but by now I'd learned to roll with it. It was sweet in his Sam kind of way.

We made our way down the carpeted atrium and slowed to a stop by my door. I jammed the key in the lock and turned, shooting him a quick glance.

"Speaking of gifts, what did you end up getting for Melanie this year?" I asked as the door swung open. We stepped in and he made a beeline for the mini-bar I'd created with a glass and iron bar cart, and festive glasses in all shapes and sizes.

Sam poured himself a glass of the whiskey I kept especially for him and gulped down two fingers of it before scrubbing a hand through his dark hair. "Doesn't matter."

"Why not? I bet she loved—"

"We broke up a few days ago," he blurted, his tone more curt than I'd ever heard it.

My shoulders fell and I plopped down onto my overstuffed, gray sofa with a sigh. Seemed like I wasn't the only one with trouble in romance-land. "What do you mean? How come?"

"It wasn't working out." He shrugged his broad shoulders and took another sip. "You want?" he asked, gesturing to the vodka bottle questioningly.

I ignored his attempt to change the subject and pressed harder. "I don't get it, Sam. Why? She was so nice. And I thought you liked her."

"I did like her. We just had some...issues."

"Like what?" I pressed.

There was a long pause and Sam used the time to inspect his drink as if it held the answers to life's most profound questions. Finally, he turned to face me. "Irreconcilable differences." The note of finality ringing in his voice was a clear indication that, as far as he was concerned, the subject was closed, but damn it, a person didn't hide things like this from their best friend for days without a good reason.

"Why are you being so closed off?" I asked gently, patting the space beside me. "Come on, it's me. Let me in, Sam."

He eyed me over the top of his highball glass, took a sip, and then let out a deep sigh. "Fine. If you swear you'll stop badgering me, I'll tell you. But remember, you asked."

He joined me on the couch, keeping a safe distance between us. "There were some issues in the bedroom."

"I...see," I said, ignoring the rush of heat that shot to my cheeks.

As close as we were, Sam and I rarely talked about sex outside of bawdy jokes. Our personal sex lives were something we both sort of tacitly tiptoed around. And now, as I was facing his head on, I realized why. Sure, Melanie was nice. But when I thought of her in Sam's bed, all snuggled up against him, with her naked bits touching his naked bits?

It made me feel all squidgy inside and I didn't like it one bit. *Another one to file under be careful what you wish for, dummy.*

"So, like what kind of problems?" I ventured finally. I'd been the one to open this can of worms and now that I'd finally coerced him into talking, it seemed only polite to make sure he knew if he wanted to keep talking, I was here for him.

"I just wanted to have sex more than she did, that's all."

"In a general kind of way or like a crazy four-times-a-day kind of way?"

He stared at me like I'd sprouted a second head.

"What? It's a serious question," I said.

"What do you take me for?" he asked, running his finger around the edge of his glass. "No, I just wanted, I don't know, a few times a week? Maybe for her to initiate sometimes?"

An image of me standing in Sam's bedroom doorway in nothing but a trench coat filled my head and I shoved it away ruthlessly.

I swallowed to moisten my suddenly dry throat and nodded. "That sounds nice, actually. And very reasonable." I patted his arm awkwardly. "Trevor never wants to anymore," I added.

Why had I even said that? It was true, but Jesus, we'd already crossed one invisible boundary tonight. It was like I was trying to make this as weird as possible for both of us.

An uncomfortable silence settled over the room and Sam took another sip of his drink, then set it down on the table next to him.

"Never? I can't imagine—" he broke off, his voice sounding low and gravelly before he cleared his throat. "Are things okay otherwise?"

"He just isn't interested for some reason."

What I didn't bother to add was that I hardly cared anymore. I had the distinct feeling that tomorrow's pro list was going to be woefully short.

Sam's gaze lingered on my face for a long moment and then he turned away. "Well, I'm sure you guys will work it out," he said, slapping his knees and shooting me a bright, forced smile. "What's tonight's movie? *To Grandmother's House We Go?*"

I tugged off the coat on my shoulders and tossed it onto the chair across from us as I stood. "Been there, seen that twice already this season. Tonight, it's *Mistle-Tones.*"

"No," Sam groaned.

"Come on, Sammy." I flicked on the TV and headed into my bedroom, calling back to him over my shoulder. "Can you get it off my Netflix queue while I change?"

I took an extra couple minutes finding my pj's because I was still feeling weird and unsettled, but by the time I went back out, I'd managed to talk myself down.

We settled in close together, ready to slip back into our more regular, comfortable routine.

Still, as the movie started, I couldn't help but think of what Sam had said.

If the amount of sex in a relationship was a deal breaker for him, maybe it should be for me, too. I lived a safe and boring life by choice. If I took sex out of the equation too, I might as well just nap for the next sixty years.

That so didn't work for me.

New top priority for tomorrow?

Find out what was going on inside Trevor's head so I could decide if a pros and cons list was even worth doing. Because that awkward exchange with my bestie a few minutes ago?

Had been the sexiest thing to happen to me in months.

Not good.

Chapter Two

Sam

It took roughly ten minutes of watching the movie before Maggie curled up in a ball, laid her head in my lap, and went straight to sleep.

Her soft brown curls were splayed across my thigh and I glanced down at her while I nursed my scotch, thinking again about what she'd said earlier.

The idea that she was sex-deprived had instantly sent my brain into overdrive and made my cock twitch with anticipation. Which was why I'd always avoided the topic with her whenever possible. It only made my balls ache and my brain throb with dirty thoughts. Better to steer clear of it altogether with her— and God only knew the last thing I wanted to hear about was what her sex life with Trevor was like.

Fucking Trevor.

I'd never liked the guy, but he'd hung around for years like a vine on a tree that was slowly sucking away its life force. Not that Maggie had changed because of Trevor. She was rock solid. The same awesome person she'd always been and her relationship hadn't gotten in the way of our friendship. It was just, well, he didn't make her happy.

Not in the way he should, anyway.

Not the way I could.

Her love of all things Christmas? Trevor hated that. He was a big Halloween guy and refused to acknowledge the season until December twenty-fifth. She wasn't allowed to watch her Christmas movies around him, either. What was that about? *Too much joy in her face for you, Trevor?* I'd always wanted to ask him snidely.

But it was more than that. When we were all out together, he was like the fun police, constantly monitoring her. Watching how much she was drinking or giving her a look if she ordered something too heavy off the menu. Maggie took it all in stride, but I noticed. Just like I noticed how he never held the door for her and never got her flowers just because.

It was the little things. And Trevor never paid attention to the little things. But now, if he also wasn't taking care of business when it came to the bigger things?

That was a serious problem. It was one thing to forget flowers; it was another entirely not to do your damnedest to make sure your woman came until she was hoarse from screaming at least a couple times a week.

Almost as if she could hear my thoughts, Maggie shifted in my lap, opening and closing her full lips in her sleep as she twisted closer to my aching crotch.

Fuck, I had to get out of here and fast—before she woke up and realized exactly what she'd done to me.

Careful not to disturb her, I slipped away from her and propped a pillow beneath her head. I padded quietly to the linen closet and pulled out a fluffy blanket, pausing to shake it gently over her before sneaking out the door, making sure to lock it behind me with my spare key.

My building was only a block away and the snow still wasn't coming down all that hard, so I opted to walk and leave my truck behind in hopes that the cold air would do me and my wayward dick some good.

Hands in my pockets, I strolled down the sidewalk, trying my hardest not to think about Maggie and Trevor, but I couldn't help myself.

For all his problems, it was nice that Maggie had someone. Someone stable and long-term. That was what I wanted, too, but for some reason, my taste in women had always left something to be desired.

They always started out normal enough. Like Fiona, the girl I'd dated over the summer. She was beautiful and smart—a kindergarten teacher with a heart of gold. Or, at least, that's what I'd thought until she'd broken out the whips and asked me to meow like a cat. I liked to get wild as much as the next guy but there was a line for me, and she was way on the other side of it.

Then there was Bethany, the short-lived brunette I'd met during a skydiving excursion. She was funny and easy to talk to, and we even shared a passion for death-defying sports. For a while I thought she might be the one that would make the dreams starring Maggie finally cease and desist. But when a waitress at a diner got a little too friendly with me one day, Bethany slashed her tires and stuffed a banana in her exhaust pipe.

When I'd confronted her about it, she'd looked me dead in the eyes and said, "Now you know not to toy with me. Next time, I'll cut a bitch."

I'd walked out of her apartment, called the cops, changed my number, and never looked back.

Which brought us to Melanie.

She'd seemed normal, just like the rest of them. She was a manager at a department store and she loved country music. On our first few dates, she'd tried to get me into the scene and I'd gone along. We had fun, teasing each other and trying new things.

She was the kind of girl that a guy could settle down with.

If, of course, it hadn't been for her sexual hang-ups.

I'd tried to be understanding at first. I knew it was awkward to be with a new person, so when she wanted to have sex with the lights off and under the sheets, I didn't mind.

But then she'd just lain there, quiet as a mouse, holding her breath like she was waiting for something painful to be over. Like having sex with me was the equivalent of having a root canal. Again, I'd put it off to nerves or insecurities. I'd tried to soothe her of them, tried to show her how to relax and let herself go, but nothing worked. In fact, it only got more difficult. On the rare occasion she wanted to have sex, she left her shirt and underwear on, insisting that I do the same and push her panties to the side. But even that only happened three times before enough was enough.

I wanted to be with someone who wanted to be with me. I didn't want to beg a woman to have sex with me, didn't want to convince her. It felt wrong and weird.

When I'd finally called her on it flat out, she admitted that she'd never had a sex drive and didn't want to pursue any type of alternative to that. She was perfectly happy living a life without sex.

I sure as hell wasn't.

But the worst part was? I wasn't even sad. In fact, I felt kind of relieved. Because if I had to sit down and be totally honest with myself, I'd have to admit that it probably didn't matter much one way or the other. Flawed or not, the reason I hadn't settled with those women or any of the rest was simple.

They weren't Maggie.

I reached the door of my apartment and shuffled inside, careful to brush the snow from my shoes and shoulders before glancing around the place.

It was everything Maggie's place wasn't. Where her house was warm and cozy, with stacks of magazines and rows of scented candles, mine was sterile and neat. There were no blankets or cupboards full of movies. But then again, that was probably because I hadn't allowed Maggie to redecorate the thousand times she'd asked.

Trudging into the kitchen, I fixed myself a turkey sandwich and carried it into my living room. Then I plopped onto the sofa and stared down at my sad, lonely meal.

Maybe I had to settle for the fact that, no matter how hard I looked, I would never find anyone that fit with me the way Maggie did. She was just...my person. The puzzle piece that clicked with mine.

She was the person I called when something good happened. And when something terrible happened, too. She was the person I could count on at the end of the day.

People could go their whole lives without finding someone as true and genuine as Maggie.

So whenever I had to entertain the idea of her fucking someone else...

I scrubbed a hand over my face.

I was losing my mind. Or, at least, I was going to if I didn't get Maggie off the brain.

Maybe it was a good thing she wasn't going on this trip with me and the guys. It would give me a chance to get my head clear and my priorities straight. They already broke my balls mercilessly when she wasn't around about how I had two girlfriends, her and Melanie, and how I'd flipped the scripts of the whole "friends with benefits" thing in the lamest way. They called it "Ball and Chain Without Benefits."

Bunch of fucking geniuses, the lot of them.

I took a bite of my sandwich before noticing my appetite was gone, then threw the rest of it in the trash before making my way to my room and opening my suitcase.

The big snowboarding and skiing trip was only a couple days away and I was going to focus on prepping for that. Grabbing some stuff from my dresser, I threw in a few days' worth of clothes, my toothbrush, deodorant, and—

I opened the top drawer and stared down at the yellow box of condoms staring back at me.

Maybe better not to bring them. I needed a break, not just from Maggie and Melanie, but from all women. A chance to clear my head and get away from wild one-night stands and the crazy that always found its way to me.

Yep, this trip—and the celibacy that went with it—was exactly what I needed to clear my mind.

So why was it that when I climbed into bed and closed my eyes, all I could see was Maggie's head in my lap all over again?

Chapter Three

Maggie

I cracked my knuckles and stared at the closed door, swallowing back the sudden rush of nausea.

Sam was right the other night and it had been keeping me awake ever since. A terrible sex life was a deal breaker. So, this morning, after letting my pros and cons list marinate for a day, I'd come to a decision. I'd give it one more shot to fix this part of my relationship with Trevor and settle on the rest if it worked out—after all, no relationship was perfect.

If this didn't work, then it was over. It had to be. I was too young to live in a sexless relationship.

Mind made up, I'd finished shopping at the farmer's market and headed over to his place with a plan—and nothing else except the lacy black thong and trench coat I was wearing.

We'd been together for a long time, and it seemed childish to give it up without a fight. But that was no excuse for losing the spark in our relationship, and if he wasn't going to be the one to put it there, then I was going to at least try to. For both our sakes.

Some part of me still felt conflicted, but I shoved it back and resolved to muscle through.

Clearing my throat, I squared my shoulders, pulled out my

key, and walked through the door—just in time to see two people tumble from the sofa onto the floor.

Two naked people.

Two *familiar* naked people, one *literally* inside the other.

Trevor and his assistant Adelaide. Jesus Christ.

My heart stopped in my chest and I clenched my fists, opening and closing my mouth a few times like a bass flopping around on a pier. Unlike in the movies, he didn't have the balls to tell me it wasn't what it looked like. He just shoved the blonde on top of him away before getting up to display his rapidly deflating penis.

"Maggie—"

"No," I said, holding up a trembling hand. "I don't even want to fucking hear it."

I wheeled around and stormed out, slamming the door behind me. I heard the door open again, heard his feet thundering after me, but I kept shaking my head and saying "no" over and over again so loud that I nearly drowned everything else out until I reached the elevator.

He was a few feet away from me with a towel around his waist that was too small for him, but before he could reach me, the elevator doors slid shut.

Pulse hammering, I winced and then leaned back against the metal walls as the cart jerked to life, speeding me down to the lobby.

"No," I said again, closing my eyes and rubbing them. "No, Jesus, no."

Was this seriously happening right now? God, it explained so much. The fact that, so many nights, Trevor had been stuck at work. The way he'd suddenly stopped wanting to sleep over on the weekends. The fact that he hadn't touched me in months.

What a fool I was, trying to fix things.

My cheeks burned with humiliation as I scurried down the

street, trying to get a head start in case he decided to get dressed and follow me.

I couldn't face him. Not yet. I couldn't call Sam, either. By now, he'd only just be getting off his flight and I sure as hell wasn't going to ruin the first day of his vacation with my breakup.

Because that's what this was.

After all these years, Trevor and I were over. All that time, wasted.

A strange sort of grief settled over me and tears stung my eyes. Weird that, even now, I didn't mourn the loss of Trevor in my life. It was the investment of time and energy and the humiliation at being played for a fool that shook me the deepest. Maybe tomorrow, when it wasn't so fresh…when I wasn't running down the street in a pair of stilettos and a trench coat, I could cling to that.

Checking to make sure my credit card and ID were in my pocket where I'd left them, I made a dash to the liquor store down the street and got myself a cart.

Tonight was a night that called for Amaretto sours and shots of tequila in between. It was a disgusting combination, but it was going to get the job done and quick.

When I'd finished getting my supplies, I went to the neighboring convenience store and stocked up on chips, pretzels, ice cream, and candy, and then hauled all my goodies to the subway.

I couldn't go home. That would be the first place Trevor would go to look for me. But I did have a spare set of keys to Sam's house, and his place was a block closer to the station than my own anyway.

Ignoring the glances of leering old men near me, I fingered the keys in my pocket and squared my jaw. I was only supposed to water the plants and check the mail, but I knew Sam wouldn't mind if I ducked out at his place for a while. In fact, if he knew what was going on, he would insist on it.

God only knew he'd hidden out at my apartment from his innumerable girlfriends over the years. Then, maybe after some ice cream and a few stiff drinks, I would be able to really process what that lying piece of shit had done to me.

Because honestly? Right now it didn't make any sense.

I was good in bed. I knew it. I was open to trying new things, was an active and vocal participant. I wasn't going to let this make me think otherwise.

And as far as frequency? It was always *me* asking *him* if he wanted to have sex lately, never the other way around. I took an interest in the things he liked, I listened to his boring work stories...

But more than that, I'd thought he was a good guy. A genuinely good guy.

But he wasn't.

The subway pulled to a stop and I gathered up my things before trudging onto the platform and making my way to Sam's place. It was easy enough to let myself in, and I set my things down on the entryway table before glancing around and allowing myself to slump against the wall.

This was exactly what I needed.

A place like Sam's—all clean, with sleek lines and modern furniture—felt like a trip to a nice hotel. Like I was on a vacation from a really shitty, depressing reality.

So that's exactly what I did. After unpacking my bags, I grabbed my favorite tub of ice cream, found the only channel still playing Christmas movies, and poured myself a drink. Tonight was a night to forget my troubles—big as they were. Tomorrow, I'd figure it out. A few hours later, I'd changed into a pair of Sam's sweatpants and an old T-shirt, managed to drink two Amaretto sours and a shot of tequila, and was feeling less angry and a little sleepy. Maybe I'd actually get some sleep tonight after all.

I said a silent prayer of thanks to Ben, Jerry, and Jose Cuervo as I blearily made my way to Sam's bedroom. He hadn't bothered to make his bed before he left this morning, but I didn't mind.

Instead, I snuggled into the space where I knew he slept, breathing in deep so I could smell his shampoo on the pillow, and closed my eyes. Sam would never do what Trevor had done to me.

Never.

I drifted off to sleep for what felt like roughly three seconds before I woke up to find my thigh vibrating and the late morning sun streaming through the window.

"What the..." I sat up, rubbing my eye with one hand as I grappled down into the sheets where my cell phone rested. I found ten missed calls—seven from Trevor, three from Sam.

Sliding my thumb over Sam's name, I called him back and pressed the phone to my ear.

"Hello?" I asked, my voice cracked and groggy.

"It's eleven there," he said.

"Yeah, yep. I knew that," I said, trying to make my voice sound less like it had just gone through a wood chipper.

"So why are you still asleep?" he asked.

"I'm not allowed to sleep in?" I asked lightly, the pounding in my head making me a little nauseous with its intensity.

"No. You never do. What's going on?"

He sounded suspicious and for a moment I fought with myself over whether to tell him the truth. One way or another, he was going to get it out of me; he knew me too well for me to lie to him for long.

"Look, could I stay at your place while you're away?" I asked.

"What? Why? Did something happen to your apartment?" he demanded, the worry clear in his voice.

"No, nothing like that. I just... I need a break for a couple of days."

"That's not cryptic or anything," Sam scoffed.

I sucked in my cheeks. *Okay, here we go. Like a Band-Aid.*

"I need to be someplace where Trevor can't find me."

The long pause echoed over the line louder than any words could.

"Did he hurt you?" Sam demanded, his voice barely more than a snarl. "I swear to God, Maggie, I'll—"

"No!" I cut in sharply, gripping the phone tighter as the shame came again in one, giant wave. "Not physically, anyway. He—we broke up."

Silence filled the line for a long moment and I glanced down at my phone, wondering if we'd been disconnected, but then Sam's voice buzzed through the line again.

"You can't stay there alone."

"Oh, don't be dramatic. It's just a breakup. I'll be—"

"You won't," he argued. "Tomorrow is New Year's Eve and you're not going to spend it by yourself. Come here with me. I'm on my laptop buying your ticket right now."

"Don't buy me a ticket. Seriously, Sam," I murmured, pressing my fingers against my aching temple.

"Too late, it's done," he snapped back. "You need to get to JFK in ninety minutes, so be quick about it. Go pack and I'll call you in a little while."

The phone went dead and I stared at it for a long moment before shoving it back in my pocket.

Leave it to Sam to hijack my plans. Still, I couldn't bring myself to be angry at his heavy-handed tactics. If the shoe had been on the other foot, I'd have done exactly the same thing.

Besides, some time with my best friend would be good for me, especially when I was hurting so badly. All I had to do was get home, pack a bag hella-fast, and hope for the best.

Three hours later, I found myself buckled into the window seat on a plane headed to Colorado with nothing but the few clean clothes I'd had in my drawers.

A magazine lay in my lap, and as I watched the people passing by, I wondered how many of them were on vacation and how many were headed home after the holidays.

Occasionally, just to keep my brain from replaying the scene from the previous day over and over on a loop in my head, I made stories for the passersby, but when an older woman in a chunky-knit cardigan stopped in front of me and flashed her ticket, I smiled and forced myself to focus.

"Looks like we're in for this trip together, neighbor," the woman said with a wink. "Did I interrupt you? You look deep in thought."

"No, uh, just distracting myself. Do you need help with your bag?"

In answer, the old woman heaved her luggage into the overhead compartment and let out a sigh. "You don't raise four boys without having a good bit of strength to back you up. But thank you."

I smiled a little more genuinely. "Four boys? I can't imagine."

"Oh yes, on my way to visit the older one now. Spent Christmas with the little one. But then, the little one is forty, so." She chuckled and then stuck out her hand as she took her seat beside me. "Agatha."

"Maggie," I said, shaking her hand. When I released it, she buckled herself in and gave me another once-over.

"What's taking you to Colorado, then, Maggie?"

"Oh, a friend. Meeting up for a ski trip," I replied.

"That's nice. Has she been a friend for a long time?"

"He's been my friend since college, yes."

Agatha nodded, her blue eyes twinkling. "And what's taking you to him? Is he getting married there or something?"

I laughed. "Oh. No. Not him. I just..." I rolled my eyes at myself, but figured I might as well tell this woman everything. We had plenty of time and, after all, it wasn't like I'd ever have to see her again.

"To be honest, I just sort of had a big breakup and he's flying me out to join him on vacation to cheer me up."

"Wow. Good friend. And he's flying you first class." Agatha sniffed. "We should all be so lucky."

"Yeah, he's a really good friend," I agreed.

"You'll excuse me, dear, for overstepping but..." Agatha paused. "You're newly single and your male friend is flying you out to join him on a vacation? Don't you think maybe..." She rose her brows and gave me a knowing look.

"I know how it sounds, but trust me, it's not like that," I reassured her with a stiff laugh.

Agatha nodded. "You know best, I'm sure. It's just not many men would spend so much money on a first class ticket to cheer up a friend."

I smiled and we fell into companionable silence as the flight attendants followed their procedure and the plane took off.

Still, as we ascended and my ears popped, I found myself glancing at Agatha every now and then, her words playing in my mind.

Sam did very well for himself as a well-known photographer, but he wasn't independently wealthy and a last-minute first-class ticket had surely cost him a pretty penny. Why hadn't I noticed that? It was possible it was the only seat left on such a short-notice flight, I supposed.

Doubt stirred low in my stomach and I settled back into the leather chair, thinking hard. Now wasn't the time to fall down rabbit holes or read into anything.

Sam had brought me out to have fun.

And that was what I was going to do.

Chapter Four

Sam

I sat in the lobby, watching droves of people in their snowsuits and ski goggles head out onto the slopes.

According to her text, Maggie ought to be here any minute, and even though my friends had headed back out after lunch like two hours ago, I wanted to make sure I was here for her when she arrived.

For what felt like the millionth time, I checked my watch and then glanced at the concierge, who had been eyeing me up and down for the past half hour. Averting my gaze, I leaned closer to the fire, warming my hands as another horde of people bustled past me with skis and snowboards in hand.

In truth, I still didn't know what I'd say or do when Maggie got here. I couldn't exactly pump her for information about whatever happened with Trevor. I was sure it would be a sore subject, and I needed to be aware of that. I also couldn't bring her attention to the one thing that had been on my mind since we'd gotten off the phone last night.

This was the first time in all the years I'd known her that she was actually single.

Sure, I'd had my stints of monogamy, but for Maggie? This was huge.

And the last thing I wanted to hear her say was how much she wanted to stay single for a long, long time. Imagining her with Trevor was one thing, but the thought of Maggie out with various Tinder dates sowing her oats and stocking up on all the screaming orgasms Trevor had neglected to deliver over the past many months made my gut clench.

I knew the things people said after breakups. That now would be the perfect time to find herself and figure out who she was without a man in her life. That this was a chance to start fresh.

But it wasn't. Not in my eyes.

This was her chance to realize what I'd known since the first moment I'd laid eyes on her.

We belonged together.

The only question was how to get her to see that.

Selfish prick.

I couldn't exactly swoop in the second she arrived, heartbroken after years of wasting her time on a jackass who never appreciated her. Still, a girl like Maggie would not stay single for long.

It was the world's most fucked catch twenty-two.

Groaning, I leaned back in my chair and scrubbed a hand over my face. Maybe my best option was to just be a good friend right now. To be there for the person who meant more to me than anyone else. Then, from there, I'd just have to let the chips fall where they may and hope to God they fell my way.

I glanced at the clock above the concierge's head and he sneered at me, but before I could do anything else, I caught sight of movement out of the corner of my eye and every cell in my body snapped to attention.

Maggie was bustling through the wooden doors with a massive duffel bag in hand and I rushed toward her.

"Hey," I said.

She grinned, but I could see the pallor of her skin and the brittleness of that smile. Shit, maybe she was more broken up about Trevor than I'd imagined.

"Hey, what are you doing here?" she asked breathlessly. "I thought you'd be on the slopes already."

"Nah, I wanted to kick back for a while and relax first. Here, I'll have the concierge send this up for you."

She didn't argue as I grabbed the bag from her shoulder, but she did eye me warily. "What gives? I told you not to wait for me. I could've just grabbed my room key from the front desk, you know."

"And then you would have done what, exactly?" I asked, raising a brow at her.

She glanced around the empty lobby, apparently speechless.

"Exactly. You'd have gone up to the room, climbed into the bed, and either hit the mini-bar, the vending machine, or both and missed the perfect slope day. No, I'm not going to let you wallow. I already know you don't want to ski, so we'll find something else to do." I gave the bag to the concierge and he carried it off without a word.

"Why can't we just take it up?" she asked.

"He'll take care of it. We'll worry about getting you settled in later. We're going to hit the ground running." I clapped my hands together in anticipation. "Tell me, what's something fun you never got to do with Trevor?"

"Well, that's a loaded question…" Her pink lips twitched and a rush of heat crept up her cheeks, sending a surge of blood straight to my manhood.

Awesome.

She'd been here three seconds and I was already half-hard.

It took every ounce of strength I had not to bend down, scoop her in my arms, and find the nearest corner to show her exactly how easy *Trevor-the-fuck-up* would be to rectify.

Instead, I chuckled at her little joke and righted the crooked knit cap on her head.

"Something we could only do here," I prompted.

"Well, I don't know what there is to do in the area," she hedged, pausing to chew on her bottom lip.

Clearly, she wasn't in the mental space to make decisions, so I took the reins. "Then let's find out. There's a village at the bottom of the hill. I'm sure there's lots of stuff to do."

"As long as we're not skiing, anything sounds good to me," she said with a shrug.

"Nope, we're going for a good old-fashioned walk." I zipped up my coat and then led her back through the doors onto the cobblestone path that led into the ski village. There wasn't much there, truthfully. Just a few little tourist spots, a spa, and some restaurants, but it was enough to get her mind off things, and that was all we really needed for today. Better yet, it looked like the inside of a snow globe. She'd love the North Pole vibe of it, I was sure.

"You didn't ask me what happened," she said quietly as we reached the end of the path and trod over the light smattering that had already recovered the recently shoveled sidewalk.

My gut clenched as I shoved my gloveless hands in my coat pockets. "It's not my place to press you, Maggie. My job is to be here for you when you're ready to talk about it." I slowed to a stop and eyed her questioningly. "Do you want to talk about it?"

She sighed, then glanced at the ski lift in the distance for a long moment before focusing on me again. "I didn't really want to, but ever since I got on the plane, it's all I could think about."

"Then shoot. Maybe talking will make you feel better." Christ knew it would make me feel better. Or, if not better, at least less tense. I was on edge, wondering exactly how bad things had gotten between them to get to this point after so long.

And, if I was being totally honest, macho bullshit or no, I

really needed to find out if I had to kick Trevor's ass when I got back to town. Because I was not opposed to a good old-fashioned throwdown.

I unclenched my fists and tried to focus on Maggie as she began to talk again.

"See, that's the thing." She wrapped her arms around her waist and shook her head slowly. "When I think about it, I don't feel anything. Like, I'm angry that I wasted my time and that he betrayed me, but as far as losing him? I'm like...numb or something."

I nodded, trying to wrangle my conflicting emotions. Numb was better than devastated or heartsick. "I can understand that. It must've been a shock if it wasn't something you'd planned to do."

"Oh, there was no plan. I stopped over there and walked in on him banging his assistant." She let out a snort. "What a cliché, right? Zero points for originality, Trevor. I have no idea how long it's been going on for. I wanted to ask but when I saw... Well, they weren't in a position to be answering questions."

"Fucking hell," I muttered through gritted teeth as I let out a deep breath. The urge to take the next plane back to New York and beat him senseless was almost overwhelming but I tamped it down. I needed to be here for Maggie right now. I inhaled deeply, nostrils flaring as my fists balled by my sides. If Trevor cheated on a woman like this?

He already had no sense.

"It's the lying that bothers me more than anything. If he wants to be with someone else, more power to him. I just don't know why he'd string me along at the same time."

I opened my mouth, closed it, then shook my head. "I'm not sure what to say. He didn't deserve you, and I'm so sorry about how it ended."

"Don't be. I was pissed off and confused and my

confidence took a serious blow, but I realized almost immediately that I never felt jealous. I wasn't broken at the thought of him with someone else. I was just…more humiliated than anything." Her eyes looked suspiciously shiny and I nodded in silence. "Anyway, I drank my way through it. Now I'm here with you, and we are going to have an amazing couple of days. Starting with checking out this adorable antique and crafts shop."

She pointed to a little hobbit-sized hut I hadn't noticed before, but I knew immediately it was her style. Advertisements for homemade quilts and candles hung in the frosty windows and I followed her as she practically sprinted toward the entrance.

"Trevor would never go in places like this. He called them granny shops."

"Then let's go in. By all means."

I motioned for her to go inside and all at once we were flooded by the smell of a thousand candles and thick, warm air.

Quilts hung from the walls and little displays of handcrafted soaps and lotions were littered through the rest of the tiny room.

Maggie wandered over to one of the quilts that was made from a soft, fluffy fabric in muted grays, creams, and pink. She ran her fingers over the intricate stitching.

"I wish I could do something like this. It's incredible," she murmured.

"Thank you, dear." A woman who looked like she'd been around for the signing of the Declaration of Independence spoke from behind the counter, and Maggie turned to face her. "You did all this yourself?"

The lady nodded, her white curls springing up and down with the motion. "Yes I did, missy. The arthritis hasn't gotten me just yet." She closed one blue eye in a broad wink.

"It's amazing. Really. You should be very proud." Maggie

grinned at her.

"You know, I bet you could learn to do it, too," I offered and the kindly old lady nodded.

"Months to learn and a lifetime to master. But you'll never be cold a night in your life." She laughed at her own feeble joke and we laughed along with her.

As they continued to talk, I walked back to the quilt and glanced at the price tag. Not cheap by any means, but given our touristy location and the quality of the craftsmanship, it seemed fair. I gathered the quilt in my arms and set it on the counter.

"I'll take it."

"Sam, no," Maggie said. "You already bought my ticket here and I can't—"

"It's not for you. It's for my place. You never have any blankets when you come over and you always love to snuggle under them. It's about time you had one," I countered.

Fact was, I'd have gotten her just about anything under the sun to see her smile again.

"But Sam..." Maggie said, but the woman behind the counter waved her off.

"You know, my mother always said to accept a gift with a smile and a hearty thank you," the old woman interjected.

I raised my eyebrows at Maggie. "See? And you always give me grief when I argue with you about the stuff you get me. Now can you please just—"

"Fine," she said with a chuckle. She rolled her eyes but grinned all the same. "Thank you."

"You're welcome." I handed the woman my credit card and she swiped it before shoving the whole of my new quilt into a bag.

This could be good and bad. A quilt like this would be a reminder of Maggie to keep in the house. Every time I looked at it, I'd think of the way her eyes had sparkled as she surveyed the neat stitching and fine seams.

Maybe I should make her take it home after all…

"There you go!"

The old woman's gravelly voice snapped me out of my daydreams and I took the bag gratefully.

"Thank you again," I said, and she nodded.

"A pleasure. Always nice to see young couples in this village. Especially a pair as perfectly matched as you two."

Maggie blinked, her eyes widening, but I just smiled and took her arm.

"Have a great day," I called back over my shoulder as I led her from the shop and out into the crisp air.

"Okay, good stop. Where to next?" I asked.

Maggie looked at me, dazed, and then shook her head and said, "Uh, I dunno…Italian food maybe? Trevor hated tomatoes. And mozzarella cheese."

A clear indicator that he was a fucking monster as far as I was concerned, but I held back the commentary, settling on, "Your wish is my command."

We followed the cobblestones deeper into the little village until we reached a strip of shops and restaurants. We checked out a couple of them from the outside and settled on a bistro tucked in the corner.

When we walked in, the scent of spicy sauce and garlic greeted us and I knew we'd picked the right place. Fires crackled merrily in every corner of the restaurant and we selected our seat near one. We'd just taken off our coats and had settled in when a smiling waitress came over and handed us some menus.

"I'll never understand that," Maggie said suddenly.

"What?" I asked, not taking my eyes from the menu.

"Why people always think we're together. You know, Trevor used to get so mad because one time when we went out with you, some woman made a comment to him about being a third wheel."

I raised my menu a little higher, careful to hide my grin.

"Yeah, it's weird, huh?"

"It's just strange to assume. I mean, we could be brother and sister."

Friend-zoned had been bad enough. And now, just when I thought there was a glimmer of hope…

She thinks of me as her fucking brother? Just kill me now.

A knife twisted in my gut but I kept my voice level. "You think so?"

"Yeah. Maybe. I don't know, it's just weird. So what are you thinking of ordering?"

In truth, I hadn't seen a single word on the menu yet and suddenly felt like the last thing I wanted to do was eat.

"I think we should start with some hot toddies," I announced, snapping the menu shut. "I ate a late lunch and I'm not that hungry."

She grinned and closed her menu, tossing it on the table next to mine. "I can definitely hold off on the food and I've always wanted to have a hot drink near a snowy ski lodge. Trevor hates snow so…"

I nodded. "You got it then."

And truthfully, after that brother-sister comment?

Alcohol was the best idea I'd had all day.

Chapter Five

Maggie

Shortly after our drinks arrived, Frick and Frack—AKA Peter and Jeremy—texted and we had them join us at the restaurant.

Together, we all decided to split a couple pizzas and, from there, the conversation fell easily into what sick moves they'd managed to pull off while they were carving through the snow.

Every now and then, Sam would shoot me a sympathetic look, knowing that I had no idea what they were talking about, but in truth, their company was a welcome break. Between what the woman in the shop had said and the lady on the plane's insinuation, my mind was going a mile a minute and I was beginning to look at Sam in a way I definitely shouldn't be.

Okay, so, yeah, he was sexy. That was a no-brainer.

I shot him a furtive glance, taking in the corded muscles of his forearms and the lock of dark hair that constantly flopped onto his forehead. And sure, he was sweet and attentive. He looked after me and made sure I always had a fresh drink and that I wasn't cold or hot. He held the door for me and pulled out my chair when we went to restaurants. Hell, he'd been looking forward to this trip for months and he'd sacrificed an entire day just to make sure I got here safe and didn't spend my time sulking.

Still, that didn't mean he had feelings for me. He hadn't argued when I'd mentioned us being like brother and sister or anything.

No, this whole line of thinking was ludicrous. Sam was a good friend. That was all…wasn't it?

After all, Trevor had loved me once and he never did any of that.

Admittedly, that wasn't the best example, but it proved my point all the same. In Sam's shoes, Trevor never would have missed the chance to hit the slopes with his friends. He hadn't even skipped the business trip that fell on my twenty-fifth birthday years back.

But Sam was there, my brain supplied helpfully.

Again, not an indication that he had feelings for me. People were just different. Sam was one of the good ones. And if he liked me surely I'd have known by now. He'd have told me or…something.

"Is that your phone?" Sam turned to me and I blinked, only realizing that I'd been so engrossed in my own thoughts that I'd totally zoned out.

"What?" I asked, confused.

"Don't you hear that vibrating noise? I think it's your phone."

I listened hard and then heard the low, gentle hum he was talking about.

"Yep, probably you-know-who again." I sighed, but fished the phone from my tiny handbag all the same on the off chance it was a family member with an emergency.

It wasn't Trevor, though. He had called—I had seven new missed messages from him since I'd left for the airport, but I also had three missed calls from my friend Deanna. I hadn't spoken to her in more than two weeks because she'd been away on a long-awaited safari, but now more than ever I really needed to hear her voice.

"It's Dee. She must be back from her trip," I told Sam. "I know the pizza will be here in a minute, but is it cool if I step out for a sec and take this?"

He waved me off. "Go give her a call and make sure she's good and all. I'll make sure these jackals don't eat all the food."

I clasped my phone a little harder as I made my way onto the fairy-lit patio of the restaurant.

Bracing myself for the cold, I sat on the iron bench against the wall and dialed Dee's number. It only took a few seconds before the line clicked to life.

"Hey," I said, trying my best to sound normal. "Everything okay? I saw—"

"What is going on?" she demanded, talking even faster than usual, which was saying something.

"What do you mean?" I asked.

"I stopped by your place to show you pics of my amazing trip and Trevor was sitting outside your door with a bunch of wilted flowers looking like a sad sack."

I pinched my nose between thumb and forefinger. "Was he?"

She hummed her confirmation. "He must have had two dozen roses and he wouldn't say a word about what happened between you guys or where you were, but I figured it wasn't good."

"Well, I can tell you that I'm in Colorado," I said.

There was a sharp intake of breath. "Like with Sam? Isn't he supposed to be in Colorado right now?"

"Yes, I'm with Sam."

"I knew it," she exclaimed, sounding oddly gleeful. "You sly little devil! So you finally opened your frigging eyes and ran away with that sexy beast and Trevor is trying to win you back? How did it happen? Don't leave a single detail out," she demanded.

My spinning mind tilted on its axis and I gripped the icy iron bench for support. "Hang on, nobody ran away with anybody," I said with a forced laugh. "I went to Trevor's apartment yesterday and found him balls-deep in his assistant."

"No," Dee gasped. "That rat bastard. I knew it. I always said—"

"You always said he was a nice guy and a great catch," I reminded her.

"To your face," Dee said casually as ever. "Because you weren't ready to hear anything else. So what, are you, like, heartbroken or—"

I rolled my eyes as I thought through my reply. "I'm getting through. Sam offered to bring me out here to get away from things for a while. I'm hoping by the time I get back, Trevor will have given up because, obviously, there is no way I'm getting back with him."

"Obviously," she agreed. "That scum. Oh, I hate men like him. They think they're so fancy with their offices and their assistants. You're better off." The words came out in an angry rush.

"Thanks, I think so too." In fact, with every hour that passed with me not missing a single thing about him, I realized it more and more.

"But let's get back to Sam," Dee pressed.

"What about Sam?" I echoed, my pulse quickening. What had prompted all that crazy nonsense she'd been spewing about us running away?

"Well, you're there with him, right? So…"

"Dee, don't be ridiculous," I snapped, my cheeks heating. "I don't know why the second I'm single the whole universe thinks I should get together with Sam of all people."

"The whole universe, huh?" Dee said, and I could hear the smile in her voice. "Tell me, has he been taking good care of you?"

I glanced through the wide glass windows of the patio and caught sight of the pair of massive pizzas being set on our table. *Saved by the dinner bell.*

"Look, Dee, I've got to go. I'll call you back the second I'm home so you can fill me in about your trip, okay?"

"Oh, no way, you chicken shit. Don't think you're getting off that easy. You guys belong to—"

In a panic, I clicked off. No way was I sticking around to listen to her conspiracy theories. Especially when they made my palms sweat and my heart race.

Instead, I rushed back inside, slipped back into my seat, took a massive hunk of cheesy goodness and slathered it with Parmesan, garlic, and red peppers.

"How is Dee?" Sam asked as he took his own piece.

"Crazy as ever," I said, and to my eternal gratitude, the conversation ended with that.

For the rest of dinner, I listened quietly while the guys planned their courses for the following day.

I managed two more slices and another toddy before we called it quits and all headed back up to the lodge. The closer I got to that sprawling beacon of light, the better I felt. I was desperate for a few minutes of alone time to reflect and refocus. Nothing like a long, hot bath to get the airplane germs off of me. After everything today? I could use a few minutes away from Sam, too.

It wasn't that he was bothering me—he never bothered me. It was just that every time I looked at him I heard the voices in my head that seemed suddenly intent on reminding me that he was a man and I was a woman. And that, when I looked at him now, I wasn't just seeing my friend Sam. I was seeing...well, broad shoulders and striking blue eyes. Shaggy brown hair and a sculpted, toned frame.

I looked away as we reached the concierge desk and sidled up next to Sam as he requested my room key.

"We'll meet up with you guys some time later or…not," Jeremy said, waggling his eyebrows before leading Peter to the elevators.

But my attention was squarely on the man behind the desk, whose face looked strange…

"I'm sorry," the man said, mouth pinched with regret as he looked up from his computer. "We contacted you back on the number provided shortly after you called us this morning. We weren't able to get you a second room."

My shoulders sagged. "No rooms?" I repeated blankly.

He looked me in the eye. "No rooms."

"Shit, I'm so sorry, Mags. My room has two queen beds," Sam said. "You can bunk with me. You'll have your own bed and we can try another place nearby tomorrow if you'd rather."

"I couldn't do that. You paid all this money for a nice vacation and now I'm—"

"Making it more awesome by being here. Don't be ridiculous." He turned to the concierge and handed him a five. "Could you please bring her bag to room 417?"

"Surely, sir." The concierge nodded and then slid another key toward us. "Your key, ma'am."

I took it, then turned it over and over in my palm, like if I just flipped it fast enough, a magic solution might appear.

But was this really a problem? I'd stayed at Sam's house a million times. I'd fallen asleep in his lap just the other night. What was the big deal with sharing a hotel room?

Yesterday, it would've been no big deal at all. Now though? When I was seeing him with new eyes? The eyes of apparently everyone around us…

It was everything.

With a deep breath, I followed Sam up the steps and down the hall until we arrived at the room. He opened the door for me and I stepped inside, glancing from the mirrored bathroom and soaker tub to the wide, queen-sized beds with homey quilted comforters. It was a true ski resort and I flopped onto the bed gratefully before glancing out the windows and catching sight of the fresh flurry of snow that had begun to fall.

"I bet they have Christmas movies still if we ask," Sam said.

I shook my head just as someone arrived and set my bag down at the foot of my bed. I thanked him, placing a discreet tip in his palm, and he disappeared with a swift nod, clicking the door shut behind him. The sound echoed through the room like a shot and my face went white hot.

"I'm going to take a shower, I think. Get the travel off of me," I mumbled.

"Okay, then. I'll be here."

I opened my bag and grabbed my pajamas before rushing into the bathroom and turning on the comforting spray. As the steam began to rise and coat the mirrors, I stripped down and then stepped into the walk-in shower. Water sluiced down my back and hair as I closed my eyes and sucked in a steadying breath.

This awkward feeling—the knot in my stomach whenever I thought of Sam lately—would pass. It was just all the influence of the people around me and the shock of Trevor's infidelity that had me reeling.

The idea of actually being with Sam...

I shook my head as my entire body tingled. It was impossible. If it didn't work out, I would be ruining one of the most important relationships in my life. I just had to remain cool, calm, and collected. Keep my head on straight. And when everything was said and done? I'd feel normal around Sam again. Just like I always did.

Or had I?

My mind drifted back to that time we went to the beach last summer and I'd caught sight of him stepping out of the ocean looking like a Greek god with his broad, muscled chest and six-pack abs. Lord knew I didn't feel normal that day. And although

I'd pretended my dream man that night had been some faceless fantasy, I was pretty sure, if I was being honest with myself, that he'd looked an awful lot like Sam.

Or when he and Melanie had first gotten together and I'd eaten an entire pint of mocha chip ice cream in one sitting because I'd felt all weird inside but couldn't put my finger on why.

I let out a muffled curse and squeezed my eyes closed, trying to make these thoughts stop.

I stayed like that for a solid ten minutes, using the breathing techniques I'd learned in yoga until I felt marginally better, then I soaped up quickly and rinsed off. By the time I stepped from the shower and climbed into my pajamas, I was ready to face him.

No big deal. It was just Sam, after all. We'd crawl into our respective beds and watch some bad movie on TV. Totally normal, just like every other night we'd spent together.

I just had to keep reminding myself of that.

Walking back into the room, I pasted on a smile and got ready to suggest a movie, only to find my gaze drawn to Sam's chiseled, naked chest. He was changing into his pajamas, too, and the low-slung fleece pants did nothing to make him look less like an off-duty superhero.

Son of a—

"Movie?" I croaked.

He grinned. "Great minds. But first, I wanted to say—I know you're going through a lot with this Trevor thing and, for what it's worth, I think you're better off. I never thought he was the one."

Are you applying for the job? I wanted to ask. Instead, I swallowed hard. "Thanks."

"I mean, he just wasn't good enough. Not for you."

I climbed into my bed and snuggled down into the pillows and then turned to look at him. The knot in my belly tightened at the solemn expression on his beautiful face.

"I appreciate that, Sam. You're a good friend."

He turned away but not before I saw a flicker of…something in his eyes.

Something that made my whole body go up in flames.

Chapter Six

Sam

If I'd thought listening to Maggie take a shower in the next room had been hard on me—literally—the next two hours were the longest of my life.

We lay just an arm's length apart as we watched some mindless movie starring Will Ferrell. Or, at least she did. I just pretended to watch it as my brain ran until there was nothing left in it but fumes.

Did she really mean that brother-sister thing?

And, if she did, then why had she been giving me looks I could only describe as hungry as the night had progressed?

Whatever the case, things were suddenly markedly different between us and I had no clue how to fix it.

Moreover, I wasn't sure I even wanted to. Throwing my name in the ring could only complicate things. And eventually, Maggie was going to get over the anger and humiliation over what happened with Trevor and then she was going to find someone new. I honestly wasn't sure I could stand by and watch it again. Watch some other guy sit around like a lump of shit while I made her smile and then watched as she went home with him.

I raked a frustrated hand through my hair and groaned.

The guys were always breaking my balls about her. About how I should just stop dicking around and make a move, but I wasn't so sure.

"I mean, we could be brother and sister."

"Fuck," I snarled and launched myself off the bed.

* * * *

After what I'd dubbed in my head as "Awkward Movie Night," I'd eventually fallen into a fitful sleep, resolving to clear the air between us ASAP, but as soon as the sun rose the next day, she was up and out, on her way to the spa. Which, I supposed, was for the best. What if I was reading into all this? So what if a couple friends and a stranger thought we should be together? If I made a move and she didn't feel the same, talk about awkward.

I could lose her altogether.

Before, it had always been easier to resist her and look but not touch. She belonged to someone else... She claimed she was *happy* with someone else.

But lately, it had been tougher and tougher. And now?

Now I felt like a cat with a ball of yarn dangling over my face, close enough to touch but still just out of reach. The timing still wasn't right, and even if it was, I had no idea if Maggie was capable of feeling about me the way I did about her.

And yet I couldn't wipe her from my mind.

As I downed a quick breakfast and hit the slopes with Jeremy and Peter, my thoughts turned to that bastard Trevor. What an ass he had been for doing what he'd done to her. How, if I was with Maggie, I'd cherish her forever. And most of all? What she'd said about it.

That she didn't miss him, wasn't heartbroken over him.

So did that mean she was willing to entertain the idea of someone new? She hadn't said any of the "time for rebirth and finding herself" things I'd expected. In fact, when it came to her love life, she hadn't said much at all.

Conflicted as ever, I tore down to the bottom of the slope a little faster than I should have and skidded to a halt just in time to cover Peter and Jeremy with a fresh wave of powder.

They dusted themselves off, glaring at me, and then I nodded toward the lifts.

"Want to try someplace new?" I said. "I'd be down to hit a black diamond over on—"

"Hang on," Peter said. "Now that we're finally just all guys here, there's something Jer and I have been wanting to talk to you about."

"Oh, yeah?" I asked, wary as I yanked one glove off with my teeth. How did I already know I didn't want to hear it?

"Yeah." Jeremy nodded. "What's the fucking deal with Maggie?"

I frowned. "What do you mean 'what's the deal?' I told you guys I didn't want her to be alone for New Year's so I invited her. She said no and then her relationship hit the skids and I didn't want her sitting home and wallowing. That's the whole story."

"Right, that's what you told us," Peter said with a short laugh as he tugged off his goggles and stared at me. "But we've been around the block a time or two and we're not buying the shit you're selling anymore."

"I don't get what you mean," I said, playing dumb and wishing I had a stick to throw to distract them.

"Maggie," Jeremy said. "You've been in love with her for years and Peter and I want to know what you plan to do about it now that she's single."

"What?" I faked misunderstanding because, seriously, them guessing at the depth of my feeling for Maggie was one thing. If they had confirmation?

I'd never get a moment's rest from their badgering.

"Look, guys, I know you want this to be like some Kate

Hudson rom-com so you can say you called it years ago, but she's just my friend."

"Which is why you keep checking your phone every five seconds to see if she's looking for you?" Peter raised his eyebrows.

"She just got dumped. I don't want to ditch her," I argued. That was rational, wasn't it? She was my guest; I had to make sure she was taken care of.

It was what anyone would have done.

"So you're telling us that you're not thrilled she's single?" Jeremy pressed.

I pulled my cap tighter on my head, making sure to cover my ears. "I'm never happy to see my friends hurt. He cheated on her. It was a shitty thing to do."

Peter and Jeremy exchanged a significant look and then blew out matching heavy sighs.

"What?" I demanded.

"Look, Sam, you're our friend but we have to give it to you straight. You're pussy whipped," Jeremy said as Peter nodded beside him. "And that's not easy to do when you're not even getting the actual pussy. Now that Maggie is finally single, you need to find a way to hook up with her or get rid of her all together. You can't be living your life waiting around for her to notice you. It's pathetic."

"Super sad," Peter agreed, absently swiping the snow from his pants.

"I'm not fucking doing that," I said. "She's my friend, that's all."

Peter gave me a slow nod. "Right, so you won't have a problem with the New Year's plans we're making, then?"

"Well, I want to—"

"Check with Maggie first," they finished for me in stereo and Jeremy guffawed.

"You need to do some soul searching, bro. We'll meet you

on Daring Cliff, okay?" They trudged toward the ski lift before I got the chance to argue and I watched them, thinking over everything they'd said.

Were my feelings for Maggie really that obvious? Was I really so transparent?

I hoped not. If Maggie had even an inkling of the things I'd been thinking about in the shower this morning? If she knew the way I'd imagined her there with me, naked in my arms as I lathered the lavender hotel shower gel over her stiff nipples and watched the sudsy water roll over her tight, lean body...

My cock twitched again at the thought and I swallowed hard before following my friends to the ski lift.

Every word they'd said had been right. Ever since the first moment I'd met Maggie in college—two weeks after the start of her ill-fated relationship with Trevor—I knew she was the one for me.

I'd been sitting behind her in Spanish class and she was scrawling her name over and over on the folder of her notebook in a million different fonts. I'd thought she was an art major and I'd craned to get a better look.

"I can take a picture if it's easier for you," she'd said without turning around.

It took me a moment to even realize she'd been talking to me.

"What?" I'd asked.

"You're a looky-lou." This time she turned, treating me to the smell of her ocean breeze perfume.

"No, I was just..."

"Trying to cheat? I should warn you, I'm not a good person to cheat off of. I can only say my name."

"Which is?"

"Me *llamo* Maggie," she said in the thickest American accent she could muster.

I grinned. "Me *llamo* Sam."

"So, Sam, you want to take a picture? It lasts longer."

For weeks afterward she teased me about me watching her, but I was transfixed by her drawings. It wasn't just her name, either. In the middle of lectures, I would find my gaze wandering down her notebook where she was sketching little songbirds in withered tree branches or cupcakes with a thousand sprinkles.

I could never understand what she got from me in return, but every day at the end of the lecture she would rip out her drawing and hand it to me.

"For you," she'd say and I would tuck it in my own folder, sure that Spanish was the best class I'd ever fail in my life.

From there, everything flowed naturally. I asked her about her drawings, and then her life, and then—when we realized we were both flailing for our lives in class—we studied together, too. We just fit together. We always had.

Like we were fated to be.

I reached the ski lift and hopped on, still deep in my thoughts.

My friends could say what they wanted, but with Maggie this wasn't just about sex. I wanted more from her than that.

I wanted everything. And if I was going to do this?

I was going to do it all the way.

Chapter Seven

Maggie

I'd spent the whole day getting my face smeared with mud, my feet soaked in steamy water, and my body massaged to the point of becoming as pliable as Silly Putty but, somehow, I still couldn't bring myself to relax.

On a physical level, my muscles were looser and my skin was smoother. But on a spiritual level? I was a frigging wreck.

My mind was just as topsy-turvy as it had been the day before. In the moments when I wasn't thinking about the odd comments everyone was making about Sam, I was thinking about Sam himself. The way the smell of his spicy shampoo clung to the air around him. The way he moved in his low-slung jeans and how, when he lifted his arms high, I would catch a glimpse of those abs and that narrow trail of hair that led from his belly button down…

And then, when I'd finally managed to force myself to stop thinking of Sam, I thought of Trevor and how he was nothing like Sam. Trevor, who'd abused my trust and treated me like a doormat to wipe his feet on and then ignore. Trevor, who was still probably sitting outside my apartment door right now, waiting for me to come out and take him back into my arms.

Which, of course, was never going to happen.

Flinging myself down onto my bed, I buried my face in the pillows and debated screaming out my frustration. None of this was going to be solved by me lying here doing nothing. I was going to have to do something to address all these new, conflicting feelings bubbling inside me... I just had no idea what.

Twisting around on the mattress, I pulled my robe tighter just as the door swung open and Sam walked in, his cheeks still slightly flushed from the chilled winter air.

"How were the slopes?" I asked, wondering if the shrillness of my voice had always been there or if I was simply overcompensating for the sudden rush of nerves that washed over me.

Either way, Sam didn't seem to notice. "It was great. Peter bit it pretty hard toward the end there."

"Perfect day, then." I grinned.

"Exactly." He pulled off his hat and gloves and tossed them on the dresser. His gaze narrowed on my face and he eyed me, his grin fading. "Hey, the guys were talking about going on a tear tonight and I was thinking it might be just what you need. Some booze, loose women, and debauchery might be a good start to getting old what's-his-name off your mind." He flashed me that signature grin I loved.

I smiled, unsure how to feel. I wanted to spend the evening with Sam, but the idea of hopping from one crowded bar to the next on New Year's Eve sounded about as appealing as gouging my own eyes out with an ice pick.

And, even if I forced myself to do it, I would just be a downer, so I settled on, "You know what? You go have fun with your friends. I think I'm in the mood for a more low-key kind of night."

Sam let out a sigh of relief. "Thank God. I was thinking the same thing. The idea of standing in line in twenty degree weather to get into a bar where I can't hear myself think is not my idea of a good time. I'm not twenty-one anymore—hell, I'm not even thirty-one anymore. I'll text them and tell them we're not coming and we can chill together."

I refused to examine what his response was doing to my pulse rate as he shrugged off his jacket and snow pants, revealing the jeans and sweater beneath.

"What kind of night did you have in mind?" I asked.

He shrugged. "Up to you. I've got to take a quick shower and warm up; I'm like a popsicle. Why don't you see what restaurants are around and make us a reservation and we'll start there?"

"Good idea," I said and he slipped into the bathroom. I opened my laptop and searched the surrounding area. This would be great. A chance to wipe away all the awkwardness that had been building between us the past couple days and to get my mind off Trevor.

In a resort town like this, nearly every place was upscale and on New Year's Eve, I knew it would be hard to get seats. I just had no idea it would be impossible.

I called every place in a fifteen-mile radius and literally every one of them was booked.

"Crap," I mumbled, my stomach grumbling as the tenth hostess hung up on me.

Feeling hopeless, I climbed from the bed and slid into the simple, long-sleeved black dress and black tights I'd brought along for tonight and ran a brush through my hair.

Sam stepped from the bathroom already dressed in a pair of black chinos and an emerald green sweater. A heavy roll of steam followed him into the room as he shot me an expectant smile.

"So, what's the plan?" he asked, finger-combing his still-wet hair. He looked delectable and it took me a second to manage a reply.

"We don't have one," I admitted with a wince.

"Everywhere is booked."

"Shoot. I was wondering if that might happen." His chiseled lips pursed. "So, let's just go down to the hotel bar and grab a drink for now while we talk it over. You game?"

"Not if we're going to drink and not eat. That sounds like a recipe for—"

"A great night?" Sam cut in.

"A disaster," I finished.

"Don't be silly. If they can't seat us for dinner, we'll get room service after and watch a movie. Come on, one drink. You have to show off that dress a little anyway."

His gaze dropped, skimming over the neckline of my dress and lower before flicking back up to meet mine. "You look great, by the way."

It wasn't the polite words so much, it was more his husky tone that had my arms breaking out in goosebumps.

I swallowed hard and croaked out a low "thank you" before following his lead into the hall.

When we reached the lobby, Sam ordered my vodka soda and a whiskey for himself and we sat and watched the droves of people strolling through the doors of the hotel, all dressed to the nines and ready to party.

"You're sure you wouldn't rather… This isn't lame for you?" I prodded.

"Hell no." Sam shook his head. "I'm telling you, the best place I could be tonight is hanging out with you."

A thrill of warmth coiled around my spine and I sat up a little straighter, taking my drink as the bartender sat it in front of me.

"You remember last New Year's?" Sam grinned.

I rolled my eyes. "How could I forget?"

I'd gone to a company party with Trevor at his insistence but he'd agreed Sam could come with us so I wasn't alone while he schmoozed with the bigwigs. He swore we'd only be stopping by to make an appearance. After two interminable hours of listening to a bunch of blowhards brag about the size of their bank accounts—and other stuff—Sam and I had snuck out to his truck and sat in the cab. For the next hour or so, we watched the fireworks explode over the Hudson as Sam played the CD of Christmas songs he always kept in his car just for me.

"I'll never understand why the *NSYNC Christmas album just screams 'Maggie' to you," I said with a grin, feeling oddly choked up at the memory.

"Because of your thing for Justin Timberlake."

"My what?" I demanded.

Sam laughed. "You have a thing for Justin Timberlake. When he got married, you were inconsolable and you always make a point of watching when he's on *Saturday Night Live*."

"I make a point to watch because he's an excellent performer!" I protested, pausing to take a long pull from my glass. "And I was not *inconsolable*, thank you very much. I just didn't see him and Jessica Biel together, that's all," I added with a grumble.

"Which you reminded me of often, and loudly."

"I still don't get it."

"Jessica Biel? I could explain it to you," Sam teased.

I rolled my eyes. "Men."

"What? She's a beautiful woman and she looks a little like you. She's got the heart-shaped face and the dark, rich chestnut hair and the almond-shaped eyes. You could be sisters."

Another shiver shot through me. Hadn't Sam just said Jessica Biel was hot? Did that mean he thought *I* was hot, too?

And there I go, reading into things again.

"So, just to be clear, does that mean you think I have a chance with Justin Timberlake?"

"You'd have to admit you're into him first." Sam clinked his glass with mine and we chattered on, teasing each other as we finished our drinks.

We wound up having two before conversation became impossible due to the crowd. I covered the tab over Sam's protests and we headed back up to the room to peruse the room service menu.

After stepping into the room, I kicked off my shoes and made my way over to the bed, where I plopped down and opened the menu, reading each option to Sam and ignoring the way my stomach growled at the mere mention of food.

"We have to get something Trevor would never let you order," Sam reminded me with a grin. A sizzle went through me at the sight and I turned away, cheeks flaming. This was getting to be a problem. If it didn't stop, he was sure to notice eventually and it would surely get in the way of our friendship.

The thought sobered me instantly and I dragged my gaze from him and focused on the menu again.

"How about lobster mac and cheese?"

"Lobster in a land-locked state in the dead of winter? I like it."

I rolled my eyes. "I bet it's amazing."

"Then get it. You can get whatever you want."

Sam ordered for us, getting a cheeseburger for himself, and I sat back and watched him as he hung up the phone. He'd pushed his sleeves up to bare his muscular forearms and I found myself in the same exact spot I'd been in less than a minute before.

A pang of warmth filled my heart and I chewed my bottom lip, trying to decide whether to tell him what was on my mind. We'd always been honest with each other before. Maybe pretending this wasn't happening would do more harm than good.

I pushed myself from the bed and grabbed my pajamas from my bag before padding into the bathroom.

"I'll be out in a few. I'm going to wash my makeup off and change for bed."

Also, by the way, I'm a big, fat chicken.

I shushed that annoying inner voice that sounded remarkably like Dee and made quick work of my dress. Once I'd changed into my usual nightwear of boxer shorts and a T-shirt, I paused to glance in the mirror, wishing I'd packed something a little sexi—

"No way," I snapped at my reflection. I wasn't about to blow up a friendship I'd had and cherished since college no matter how squishy Sam was making my stomach feel lately.

"Did you say something?" he called back.

"Nope, sorry. Just um…talking to myself." *Good save, genius.*

I blew out a sigh and washed my face before patting it dry and going for a second attempt at a pep talk in the mirror.

"Just because your relationship blew up does not give you the right to shift everything between you and Sam. Get it together, woman," I hissed.

My reflection nodded back at me and, together, we turned off the bathroom light and made our way back into the bedroom with a smile.

"What's up?" Sam asked, brows draw together quizzically the second I walked in. "You've been in there forever and now you've got your serious-thinking face on."

"I do not," I laughed.

"Don't lie to me about your thinking face," he shot back in mock anger.

I sighed and then shrugged. If anyone knew I had a tell it was Sam. "Fine, you caught me."

"And what are you thinking so hard about?"

"I just… I want to thank you, I guess. For being my knight in shining armor all the time," I said, knowing I was hedging, but unable to make myself tell him the full truth. "It feels like every time I need you, you're there for me and I… I can't tell you how much it means to me."

"Don't be silly, Mags," he replied, brushing me off with the easy warmth that came so naturally to him.

"It's true," I insisted. "Remember when my cousin was getting married and Trevor bailed on me at the last second? You stepped in and helped. And when my tire exploded in Maryland? You drove all the way from New York just to help me. Not everyone would do something like that."

"For you they would," Sam said, his blue eyes suddenly soft as he gazed at me.

My heart froze in my chest as our gazes collided and I swallowed hard, suddenly overcome with a rush of emotion that knocked me on my ass.

It wasn't just a look of friendship or even devotion.

No, the warmth in his gaze held so much more than that, and even without being able to see myself, I knew my eyes looked the same. A war waged inside me as I tried to think of what to do. But then, just as I was about to speak, a knock sounded at the door.

For what felt like an eternity, he didn't move and I stayed rooted to the spot, knowing the second the moment passed it might never come again. But then the pressure and tension overwhelmed me and my mouth was moving before I could stop it.

"I-I think our food is here."

There was no mistaking the disappointment in his eyes as he nodded and moved toward the door without another glance my way.

I'd blown it. What might have been my one chance to see if what I was feeling for Sam was real, and I'd chickened out.

Already the regret tasted bitter in my mouth.

Chapter Eight

Sam

Son of a bitch.

I'd been hungry. Starving really, but after what had felt like something…a real moment with Maggie, I was left hard and wanting and not a little confused as I moved toward the door. I knew what I wanted, and food was not it.

Saved by the bell? This had been more like cock-blocked by the knock, and I had half a mind to contact management.

I swung the door open and a smiling waiter greeted me.

"Happy New Year, sir!"

I instantly felt like a piece of shit for placing blame when it belonged squarely on me. I'd had more than one opportunity to tell Maggie how I felt and instead I tiptoed around it like a parent playing Santa on Christmas Eve.

No more.

I stepped aside and let the waiter roll the cart in, but my mind was elsewhere. The next opening I got, I was going to go for it. If she shot me down, so be it, but at least I could say that I tried. And if the way she'd looked at me earlier was any indication, I had a better chance than I'd thought.

"I have lobster macaroni and cheese, a cheeseburger with the works and fries, one chocolate pot de crème, a strawberry cheesecake, and a bottle of Prosecco. Is that correct, sir?"

I nodded and took the proffered bill, signing my name with a flourish and adding a twenty-five percent tip to the total.

"Thanks and have a great holiday," I said, walking him to the door.

By the time I turned around, Maggie was already peeking under the silver domes, groaning at the food porn.

"You called back and got dessert and champagne?" she asked, her cheeks pink with pleasure, making the afterthought feel like a total win.

I shrugged. "It's New Year's. We've gotta have champagne."

I moved to stand beside her and breathed in deep. The buttery, salty smell of Maggie's food overpowered my burger and my mouth watered just thinking of the meal to come. Settling the trays on the small round table in the corner, I passed Maggie her cutlery and gestured to the cheesy dish as we took our seats.

"I'm definitely trying that," I warned her.

She laughed. "Good, because I was planning on having half your burger anyway."

"Deal," I said.

She cut the bun in half then placed her portion on the plate in front of her before setting the rest in front of me.

I popped the bottle and then poured equal measures into the glass flutes between us.

"I feel like a princess. Room service and champagne. Pay-per-view." She clinked her glass against mine. "This is the good life."

I grinned. "Nothing but the best for my best girl."

I swallowed hard, noticing not for the first time that Maggie's gorgeous, trim legs were bare. It was distracting, and every time she moved I caught another flash of her creamy skin.

Forcing myself to focus on our food, I dug my fork into

her mac and cheese and took a bite. The buttery succulence of the lobster exploded in my mouth, only slightly tempered by the soft, creamy cheese.

"That's amazing." I pointed to the plate with my fork.

Maggie took a bite, her eyes rolling back as she let out a little moan of approval. My cock twitched at the sound and the look of sheer satisfaction on her face, but I shifted in my seat and took a bite of my burger.

Even now, in spite of my decision, I couldn't help but wonder what would have happened if the food hadn't come when it did. If that soft look in her eye would have stayed there as she crossed the room toward me.

In my mind, she'd lift her arms high as she tugged the belly-baring T-shirt over her head and let it drop to the floor. Then we would be past the point of no return, finally both ready to admit the thing I'd known for nearly eight years now.

That we were made for each other.

"You know what I don't get?" Maggie's voice dragged me from my thoughts and I glanced up at her.

"What?"

"You broke up with Melanie without mentioning it to me at all, but I break up with Trevor and suddenly the whole world stops."

I blinked, focusing in on her more intently. This might take some explaining and *"I never really cared about any of the girls I've been with since the day you and I met"* seemed like a little too much right out of the gate. Instead, I popped a fry into my mouth and tried to stay nonchalant. "Well, eight years and six months are pretty different breakups."

"Yeah, but it wasn't like that with Yolanda. Remember, we went bar hopping and got drunk in the movie theater when you broke up with her?"

I rolled my eyes. "We were still in college. To be fair, for a while there, I thought she could be the one."

"And why wasn't she?"

"Other than the fact that she dumped me?" I shot back.

Maggie's brow furrowed in confusion. "She dumped you? You always told me—"

"I know. Shit." I let out another low oath under my breath. This wasn't how I'd planned for things to go, but I couldn't lie to her either. Not anymore. "Yeah, she dumped me."

"What?" Her eyes shot wide as she held a forkful of lobster aloft. "So you don't have a perfect 'never been dumped' record after all?" she demanded.

I raised an eyebrow and shrugged. "Guess not. Shame, right?"

"So why did she dump you? Did she at least give you a reason?"

I hedged. "That's sort of why I...intentionally lied. I didn't need you fighting her."

"Fighting her?" A laugh burst from her lips. "Was it really that bad?"

"Depends. She said she wasn't interested in playing second fiddle to you."

Maggie's fork clattered into the bowl. "Second fiddle?" She blinked, shaking her head slowly. "She didn't play second fiddle to me. I've always been really respectful of your relationships."

"Don't feel bad, Mags. I know you've always been really considerate. Her problem was with me, not with you. She just thought..." I tried to find the right words. Ones that wouldn't scare her away. But there was no other way around this. "She thought you came first for me. Over her."

Maggie picked up her fork again, studying it like it held all the secrets of the universe. "I guess I can see leaving someone for that reason. Still, I liked her and I'm sorry she felt that way."

I shrugged. "She wasn't the one, Mags. She wasn't serious enough and she was shallow."

Maggie took a bite of her burger and groaned.

"Oh my God, that's incredible," she murmured, her mouth still partially full as she chewed. "Did you try that?"

I laughed. "Yeah, pretty good, right?"

"Better than sex," she said, leaning over to get a bigger bite and giving me a clear shot down the front of her V-neck.

I glanced away, not wanting to intrude on her privacy, but as her delighted sounds of culinary rapture filled the room, I shifted in my seat trying to quell the ache inside me—the need to hear her moaning and gasping for me instead of some second-rate cheeseburger.

"Have you thought any more about hitting the slopes?" I muttered, grappling for a safe topic of conversation.

She shook her head, straightening again. "No way. I stand by my decision. Skiing is a death trap."

"I think you'd like it if you just gave it a chance."

"There are a lot of things I might like that I'll never try. Sky diving. Base jumping. Swimming with hungry sharks."

"Why do the sharks have to be hungry?"

"Because what's the fun of well-fed sharks?" she shot back. "But, on that note, that reminds me." She pushed away from the table, food forgotten, and rose to her feet. "I brought something with me. I know you said I should wait until your birthday and all, but, well, now it's sort of a thank you gift. For everything you've done for me. And it kind of makes more sense to have it now than later."

She rooted around in her bag and pulled out a red gift bag with crisp blue tissue paper.

"New York Giants' colors." I smiled.

"Always." She handed the bag to me. "Now open up. I think you'll be able to use them."

I sifted through the tissue to find a brand new pair of ski gloves and a matching knitted hat, both in blue and red—my team colors.

"I was thinking you've had your other set for a long while

and you might need something new. The gloves are supposed to be the top of the line and I, uh, knitted the hat."

"Shut up," I demanded, staring at the hat in my hands in genuine awe. It even looked like a hat, sort of. And given the fact that Maggie had been attempting to learn to knit since the day we'd met, with a closet full of failures that could have graced even the most horrific Pinterest "nailed it" board to show for it, I knew exactly how meaningful this gift was.

I stood and took her in my arms without a second thought. "This is amazing. Thank you."

Her arms snaked around my waist easily, filling me with her warmth as she lay her head against my chest.

"No, thank you, Sam. I don't know what I'd do without you."

She pulled back a little and looked up into my eyes. That same softness from before had returned and my heart ticked faster in my chest, sending blood thrumming to my ears, my wrists, and lower.

"S-Sam?" she murmured, her voice little more than a whisper, and in that moment I knew this was my chance.

Bending low, I cupped her cheek with one hand and brought my mouth close to hers. She didn't pull away, and taking it as a sign of approval, I pressed my lips to hers.

The kiss was hesitant at first. Searching. A question more than an answer, but as her lashes fluttered closed, I wrapped my arms around her tighter.

And in that moment? It was everything and more. All the fantasies I'd had over the course of all those years sprang to life as she fell apart in my arms, pliable and responsive and sweet. Her tongue swept out to meet mine and I groaned as need pulsed through me.

I pulled her closer, angling my body against hers, reveling in the feel of her soft curves pressed against me. Jesus, she felt just like I knew she would. Like the missing puzzle piece in my life.

Like she was meant to be in my arms. Like—

A shrill sound rent the air and, for a second, I thought it was just the blood rushing in my ears. But as it continued, I realized it was a phone.

Maggie's phone.

I pulled away and she stared up at me, eyes wide, breath coming from us both in gasps.

A second later, the ringing stopped but the damage was done. I'd awakened from what felt like a dream and had been hit in the face with a dose of reality.

All of a sudden, after years of waiting, Maggie wanted to kiss me and I just accepted it. It was like I'd never seen a rom-com before. Never witnessed a rebound in action. But here I was, the big, lovable friend, setting myself up for an audience-groan-worthy fall. And I had no one to blame but myself.

"I'm sorry," I said, my voice still raspy with unquenched need. "I… I need a minute."

Shoving my hands in my pocket, I tore from the room just as quickly as my legs would carry me, leaving an open-mouthed Maggie in my wake.

Chapter Nine

Maggie

I shot a glance at the clock and groaned, flopping back onto the bed.

What had happened? I mean, I knew what had happened. Sam had kissed me and then the phone interrupted us, but dang it... Why did he have to leave?

Sick of staring at the door and waiting for it to open, I clicked on the TV and watched the crowd of onlookers in Times Square.

There were exactly twenty minutes left until the ball dropped. The only question now was whether Sam would still be gone when it happened. After all, it had already been almost half an hour since he'd rushed out of here like his ass was on fire.

I guess I couldn't blame him. It had blindsided me too.

The passion and intensity in that kiss were almost overwhelming.

The words of everyone who'd spoken to me in the past few days flooded through my mind. The woman on the plane, the lady in the shop, even my own best girlfriend. They'd all been able to see something I hadn't.

And now that it was here, staring me in the face?

I couldn't figure out how I'd never noticed it before.

The way Sam looked at me, the way he attended to me and kept me safe. The way he made me laugh. Now that we'd kissed? It seemed so obvious that we were two halves of one whole and I had just been too stupid—or too distracted—to notice. Yolanda, Trevor, Dee…probably even Frick and Frack a few rooms down the hall knew it before I did.

But now that I knew? Now that I sat here with the imprint of his warm lips still searing into my skin? I didn't care about anything else. I just wanted to make up for lost time.

The rest of my worries had been burned into oblivion by the heat between us. I no longer cared how this would affect our friendship, or how I'd wasted eight years when the right man had been in front of me all along. I wanted Sam and the only questions that remained were where he'd gone, when he'd be back, and, most importantly, if he'd kiss me like that again.

Heart thrumming in my chest, I grabbed my phone from the bedside table and stared down at the number of the missed call.

Fucking Trevor, still messing my life up, only long distance now. I thumbed past his name and typed Dee's number into a message.

Sam kissed me.

I stared at the simple words, my heart leaping like I was sixteen again and kissing was the most wonderful thing I could imagine.

With a deep breath, I sent the message, and then flopped back onto the bed and stared at the ceiling.

Not even a solid ten seconds passed before my phone rang.

Taking it in hand, I pressed the glass screen to my ear and winced as Dee shrieked over the line.

"Oh my god! You two idiots finally figured it out! I knew it, I knew it would happen. Tell me, did you kiss him back?" she shouted with excitement.

"I did," I said, trying to sound much calmer than I felt.

"And?" Dee asked "How was it?"

"It was..." I couldn't help it. I actually squealed with delight. "It was incredible. It was so tender but firm and sexy and... I don't know. It was just so Sam."

"I'll bet it was." I could hear Dee's smile in her voice. "So the real question is why are you wasting your time calling me? Don't you have some, you know, business to attend to?"

"That's the thing, the second after we kissed, he rushed out of here like he was Bruce Wayne and just caught a glimpse of the bat signal blinking in the distance."

"Cold feet?" Dee said, sounding perplexed.

"I have no earthly idea. That's why I was calling you," I countered with a pained laugh. "I think he feels like it was a mistake, maybe."

It wasn't until I said the words out loud that I realized how much that thought terrified me. What if that was it? What if it felt wrong to him, despite me knowing nothing had ever felt so right?

"Just, you know, give him a second to process. This is new for both of you. He was probably resigned to you and Trevor and now all of a sudden, you guys are breaching the friendship barrier and making out. He'll figure it out soon enough. When have you ever known Sam to not do the right thing?"

"And the right thing is...?" I asked.

"Getting back in that ski lodge and not leaving the bed until you've created enough heat to melt that dang mountain," Dee said with a laugh. "Trust me. He'll be back."

We said our good-byes, but even after we hung up, I held Dee's words close to my heart, like a secret wish.

He'll be back.

I had to hope she was right.

And when he got here?

This time, I'd be ready for him.

Chapter Ten

Sam

What the fuck was I doing out here?

Aside from freezing my nuts off, that is.

From the hotel's rooftop, I stared out at the snowcaps in the distance, my breath a white fog in front of me. I was standing here with my hands shoved in my pockets like an idiot while the girl of my dreams sat in a hotel room a few floors away probably wondering what the hell had just happened.

The sound of laughter broke into my thoughts and I shot a glance down at the crowd of twenty-somethings moving from pub to pub, probably in search of that midnight kiss or a quick lay.

That had been me, once. I'd been one of those guys surfing for quick, easy fun and meaningless sex to fill the time. But now?

It was the last thing on my mind.

The second I'd touched Maggie I knew I wouldn't be able to stop myself until I had her. The need was all-consuming and it scared the ever-loving shit out of me.

Which, I supposed, was the real reason I'd ended up on the roof.

I'd crossed the line and shown her my true feelings, and

whatever happened next was going to affect our relationship for the rest of time. What if this was just a moment of weakness for her? What if we took that next step and then, tomorrow, in the light of day, she was filled with regret?

It would kill me.

This was a terrible idea. The second our mouths touched, I knew it. If I loved her before, the way our bodies fit? The things those lips made me feel and want? It was a whole new level. Which meant, if it went bad, I was going to be in a world of pain. The kind that dragged you down into a deep, dark depression where you knew no one would ever compare.

The wind kicked up and I shuddered, squaring my shoulders against the gust.

What was she thinking down there all alone? She was probably as confused as I was. She'd always been the cautious one, running the numbers, checking the stats. I was the daredevil, and Mags was the angel by my side, making sure I was careful.

It was only then, as I stared out at the sheer wall of ice—a double black diamond—that I'd skied down earlier that it hit me like a load of bricks right in the gut.

What the actual fuck was I doing out here? When had I ever let fear hold me back? I was the guy who didn't want to miss a thing. A risk-taker. And instead of taking the most important risk of my life, I was here in the cold on New Year's Eve instead of telling the woman I loved how I felt.

And even better? Based on the way she'd kissed me? I had a real chance of having everything I'd ever wanted.

Maggie, totally mine.

That kiss, hot and sweet as it had been, solidified everything for me. Maggie wasn't just some girl I'd lusted after. She was my forever. And the longer I stood here, the longer I was giving her time to second guess what I knew to be true—that we belonged together. She was willing to risk it. I'd never forgive myself if I was the one who chickened out.

A man on a mission, I headed back into the warm hotel and rubbed my hands together before punching the down button outside of the elevator. I had no idea what I was going to actually say once I got there—after all, if I hadn't figured it out in eight years, I certainly wasn't going to tonight. Whatever came out, came out. Consequences be damned.

The elevator door chimed and I made my way to the room, tugging the room key from my pocket. I swiped and stepped inside, knocking gently as I did so as not to startle her.

It didn't matter though; she was reclined on the bed but her eyes were locked on the door. Our gazes collided instantly. Her eyes widened as she surveyed me, then she offered me a timid smile.

"You're back." she said.

She'd changed from her boxers and T-shirt into the hotel robe and for the life of me, it was all I could do not to cross the room and fling the terry cloth to the floor. But we needed to talk first.

I let out a deep breath. "Look, I want to apologize."

"You don't need—"

"I do, though. I'm sorry for the way I acted."

Maggie looked taken aback for a moment, but then she slowly nodded, her face tinged with a sadness that was like a punch to the gut. "No, no, really, it's okay. I totally understand. Weird moment. New Year's and all… It can do that to a person. We can just forget it ever happened and go back to the way things were. It's okay."

"Go back to…?" I frowned at her, stomach clenching as each word she'd said was like a nail being hammered into my coffin. It took me a second to realize—or hope, at least—that she'd misunderstood me. "Oh, no, Mags. I'm not sorry for kissing you. I'm sorry I left you here all this time while I thought about it."

I stepped a little closer to the bed. "The real question is, are you sorry I kissed you?"

She rolled the tip of her tongue over her bottom lip and then shook her head again. "No, I'm not. But, if you don't regret it, then why did you leave?"

I speared a hand through my hair. "Because you're not someone I can just fuck once and be okay with it. You're…everything. And the longer I kissed you, the harder it was going to be to control myself. I don't want to rush you. You just had a breakup. This…the feelings between us? It's all new for you."

"That's okay, though. We can work through it together. It's new for both of us," she corrected, the sadness beginning to lift from her eyes.

I threw back my head and let out a harsh laugh. "Not."

"What are you saying?" she asked, her brow knitting in confusion.

It was my leaping-out-of-that-plane moment, and I wasn't going to blow it this time. "I'm saying that I have loved you every second of every day since you first passed me your drawings in Spanish class."

She laughed at first but then when she saw my solemn expression, the laughter died and the truth dawned in her eyes. "Sam… That was eight years ago."

"I know exactly how long it's been." I took another step toward her and tugged her to her feet, sweeping her into my arms until her breasts were pressed tight against my chest. "I know exactly how many nights I spent with you in separate beds. I know exactly how many mornings I woke up without you by my side. And, what I'm saying, Mags, is that I'm done waiting."

Burying one hand in her hair, I leaned down and planted a soft kiss on her lips, loving the feel of her tongue as it swept out and begged me for more.

I shook my head. "I can't make love to you tonight until I know where you stand."

She searched my gaze. "I'm in shock, to be honest." She chewed her bottom lip and I could feel her body trembling against mine. "Knowing that you're...that you... All this time? And I never knew. Plus, things just ended with Trevor. How could I have been so blind? What if I fuck this up?"

This was the Mags I knew. Cautious Maggie. Careful Maggie. But if ever I needed her to trust me, it was now.

"He wasn't right for you." I gestured between us and ran my thumb over her bottom lip. "This is right."

"I think I know that," she murmured. "At least, I know it feels so natural. So obvious. I guess I'm just scared."

"Of what?"

"Me. And you. These feelings." She shook her head. "There are so many things that I admire...that I love about you. Your talent and your sense of adventure and the way you look after me. You're a better man than I deserve."

"Nobody on earth is good enough for you." I kissed her again, this time allowing her to swirl her tongue with mine so I could taste the sweet champagne on her breath. And as soon as we fell into each other's arms?

There was no way we were stopping this time. Slowly, she guided me back toward the bed and, as her knees buckled against the mattress, I asked her again. Once more for good measure.

"What do you want, Maggie?"

"You, Sam. Always you."

Chapter Eleven

Maggie

I kept waiting for it to be awkward. For one of us to laugh uncomfortably or for my fingers to shake as I moved to untie the knot that held my robe together. Instead, though, everything felt...perfect.

Like this was a moment we'd been building to for years now, a rhythm we'd already learned.

With Sam's dark blue eyes on me, I felt safe and admired and sexy in a way no man had ever made me feel. And, as he dropped to his knees in front of me, my breath caught and I knew that this was what I wanted, what I craved more than anything else in the world. To be with him. Totally and completely with him.

He pushed my fumbling fingers aside, taking the belt of my robe in his sure grip and loosening the knot with focused precision. Before he slid the white terry cloth from my shoulders, he pulled his own shirt from over his head, treating me once again to the view of his perfectly sculpted chest.

"You're incredible." The words slipped from my lips and he glanced up at me again, a soft smile on his full mouth.

"Not half as incredible as you. Come here."

Heart pounding in my throat, I nodded and his calloused

fingers brushed the space between my breasts, pushing my robe aside until it was a puddle on the bed and I was laid bare to him. The chill of the hotel room did nothing to cool the fire in my cheeks, but as Sam stared at me, I took another deep breath and readied myself for him.

"God, you're even more gorgeous than I imagined." His fingertips brushed my collarbone, the curve of my breasts, my stiffened nipples, and the plane of my stomach like he was studying a fine work of art. I shivered with need, the warmth of his skin searing against my body and making me beg for more.

But I knew, like so much of the rest of our relationship, this would take time. That this was only the beginning.

Sam stood again. "Don't move. I just want to look at you," he whispered.

I swallowed hard, the heat of his gaze giving me courage. "All of me?" I asked, lying naked before him.

Sam's heavy gaze wandered even lower, and his pupils dilated at the sight. He offered me another pained smile. "Damn if you aren't the sexiest woman alive. But I feel like I'm behind. I need to catch up."

At first, I didn't understand what he meant, but then he stood and reached for the button of his jeans. He unfastened it quickly before pulling down his fly. With one steady motion, he pulled down his boxers and pants and allowed his massive length to spring free.

Holy shit, Sam is hung.

My breath caught again. He wanted me, that much was clear, but I'd never been with a man so...big before in my life.

My mouth watered and I licked my bottom lip before leaning into him, ready to take him in my mouth and tease his swollen head with my tongue.

"What do you think you're doing?" he muttered through gritted teeth. "I told you to stay put."

"But I want to..." My voice broke and I looked again at his

throbbing shaft.

He shook his head. "Not tonight, beautiful. Tonight, I want to do all the things I've wanted to do for the past so many years, and I refuse to let you take that from me. Now get on the bed and spread those thighs apart for me again."

Blood thrumming in my ears, I did as I was told, practically quaking with anticipation.

"Scoot down to the bottom of the bed and open your legs. Like this." He closed a hand over my thighs and guided me down the cool mattress and then pushed my legs apart with his rough palms. I gasped at his sure grip…his knowing touch.

This was going to be good. So good.

He sank to his knees again and I could feel the heat of his breath on my skin.

"What are you…?" I asked, raising up on my elbows to catch sight of his solemn expression.

"I want to taste you," he said simply, and, to prove his point, he dropped his mouth to the inside of my thigh and sucked the space there until he released my skin with a gentle *pop*. His tongue peeked out as he licked and nibbled my inner thigh, over and over, moving closer to my core with every pass. I couldn't help it; by the time he was just an inch away, my hips began to pulse. I'd never felt so wild. So achy.

He let out a low groan. "Can you be patient for me, baby?" he asked, his voice grittier than I'd ever heard it before.

My body roared with need, but I gave him another nod. "I can be patient."

"Good." And, as a reward for my compliance, he lapped my center oh so gently with his tongue, making me throw back my head as my knees quaked.

My channel was pulsing, begging to be filled, and as he teased me I closed my eyes, focusing only on his tongue as he moved up and down, teasing me before finally closing his lips over that pulsing bundle of nerves. He swirled the tip of his tongue around me, growling with satisfaction as he went, building the fire inside me to a roar.

"This is perfect," I murmured breathlessly. "You are perfect."

"You have no idea how long I've wanted to do this," his gruff voice replied, and I weaved my fingers in his shaggy brown hair as he dipped low again, loving every inch of me with his tender caress. "How many times I've dreamed of this."

"God, you taste amazing," he added before moving his tongue against me in a fast, flicking rhythm.

"I just want you inside me, Sam. I'm going crazy," I rasped.

In answer, he pushed one long finger slowly into my waiting heat, releasing some of the growing tension. It was something, but not nearly enough, and my hips bucked, trying to force him deeper.

"Yes," I hissed, and he pushed into me over and over again, matching his rhythm with the movement of his tongue. "You're so good at this."

With every stroke, I took a step closer to the edge, ready to jump off into the abyss of my release, but it was too good, too right to end so soon. When I came, I wanted it to be with Sam inside of me, wanted him to feel every ebb and flow of my body as I came undone in his arms.

"I need you," I said, pulling his hair a little as I bucked into his touch. "Please, Sam, I need you inside me."

He pulled away, his eyes soft as he studied me.

"Lie back on the bed, beautiful," he commanded, and I did as he said, scrambling back toward the pillows as he got to his feet.

"You're sure you're ready?" he asked, and again my gaze fell on his huge length, swollen and waiting for me.

I nodded. "Just go slow with me. You're, um, much bigger than I was expecting…"

A lazy smile overtook his face, and his right hand snaked

down to grip his shaft, stroking once, slowly. "I'll go as slow as you need me to."

Sam joined me on the bed, and then hesitated. "Fuck," he cursed under his breath.

"What's wrong?" I asked, panicked. He hadn't changed his mind, had he?

"I didn't pack any condoms."

All the breath left my lungs in a soft sigh of relief. "I'm on birth control."

His eyes lit up and the pulse in his neck pounded visibly. "And you're sure you want to—"

"I'm sure. I need you, Sam. I want all of you."

His eyes seemed to get that much darker as he got closer.

I spread my legs wide for him again as he positioned himself between my thighs.

"You're gorgeous down there," he murmured. "So pretty and pink and wet."

"All for you," I whispered.

Gripping himself, he pushed inside me inch by agonizing inch until he was buried to the hilt. It was a shock at first, and my body clenched him tight as it struggled to accommodate him, but it didn't take long before the borderline pain became pure, needy pleasure. I let out a hiss of satisfaction, loving the fullness and completeness of feeling him inside of me, of knowing nothing was between us.

Holy shit, sex had never felt this good, and he wasn't even doing anything yet. We just fit together, it seemed.

Holding nothing back, I wrapped my legs around him, flexing my hips along with his at every gentle thrust. The motion rocked me to my core, slowly driving me wild.

I wanted more, needed more, but I knew Sam would have it no other way. With me, he wanted to take his time, enjoy my body, and I wanted to enjoy his.

I loved the weight of him pressed down on me, the way my

breasts felt against his hot chest, the way my arms felt as I wrapped them around his neck. I fell into the sweet sensation of his kiss.

I had no idea how long we went on like that, kissing and rocking together, loving every peak and valley of our desire, but after what felt like hours, Sam nipped the shell of my ear, his motions getting faster, his thrusts deeper…harder.

"Fuck, you feel so good," he grunted. "Can't wait much longer. You going to come for me?"

I gasped, heat pooling in my belly and spreading outward.

"Sam, I—"

But words became impossible as my body instinctively strained for the climax so close at hand.

"Yeah, that's it."

I nodded frantically, closing my eyes, my walls quaking as he took total command of me, pushing my body to the limit as our hips slammed together, long, hard strokes that became wilder with every second.

And then I was over the edge, careening into the abyss as the knot in my stomach loosened and waves of pleasure rolled over me like a tidal wave. Lost in the ocean of my own release, I pulled him closer as he softly groaned my name and then stiffened above me, filling me in hot, needy spurts. My world seemed to shatter as my ears rang and my body ached with the sheer bliss of release.

All too soon, it was over, and we lay in each other's arms, panting.

"Wow," I whispered. And damn, did I mean it. We'd barely scratched the surface, hadn't even learned one another's bodies yet, and it was still the most sublime experience of my life.

Because I was with Sam.

"Happy New Year," he whispered and then leaned in and kissed the tip of my nose.

"Happy New Year," I replied, snuggling close to absorb the

comforting warmth of his body.

He glanced at the clock. "It's twelve forty."

"We missed it, I guess."

"Did we? I'm thinking we probably rang in the New Year in the best possible way," he said with a grin.

"Yeah," I agreed, tracing the muscles of his chest with my fingertip. "Me too."

"Do you know I love you, Mags?" he said, his eyes full of that love.

I nodded, tears prickling the back of my eyelids. It took me a second to reply past the lump in my throat. "I do. Do you know that I love you too?"

"I do now," he said, the beaming smile on his face sending a thrill through me.

This year's resolution?

Waking up to that smile for the rest of my life.

Epilogue

Maggie

For months afterward, like the nervous Nellie I was, I waited with my metaphorical fingers over my eyes for things to get awkward. As if, one moment we might look at each other and suddenly be filled with regret or longing for the way things used to be.

But no matter how often I looked, that feeling never came.

Every day with Sam was better than the last and all the things I'd loved about our friendship before were made that much better by spending more time together and falling easily into each other's arms. In the span of two months, we moved in together, splitting my eclectic cozy style with his sleeker taste, and by the end of a year, we were married.

Or rather, on New Year's Day of the following year.

And now, here we were, on vacation for our second anniversary, carrying our luggage through the warm Hawaiian breezeways as we headed to our room.

"You're sure you wouldn't have rather gone someplace cold?" I asked. It was our first vacation since our honeymoon, and back then we'd revisited Colorado—though we'd spent most of our time holed up in the lodge. My skin still tingled at the memory.

"Positive. I think you've had to deal with enough of my snowboarding for a while."

I breathed a sigh of relief. It had been hard enough as his friend to watch him careening down the mountain like a lunatic when we were merely besties. As his wife? It was almost unbearable.

But I did it and never complained…well, hardly ever. Because that same wild spirit was what had earned us this happiness. And man, was it good.

I glanced around, checking out all the vibrant potted hibiscuses and breathing in the scented air.

I couldn't deny though, a little twinge shot through me as I thought of the city streets glittering with snow back home. It had been a dry year so far, and we hadn't gotten even an inch until the moment our plane took off. Now, New York looked like it was covered in spun sugar and I was just a teeny bit envious.

I shoved the thought aside with an internal eye roll. We'd have years of winter together and all I needed was Sam. Combined with a margarita on the sandy beach, and it would be paradise.

"I have a little surprise for you," Sam said as we reached the floor of our hotel room.

My face fell at his words. I hadn't gotten him a damned thing. "I thought we agreed—"

"We always promise no gifts," he cut in with a laugh. "And you always get me gifts anyway. But this time? I think I may have finally topped you."

"Do you now?" I raised my eyebrows.

Sam made his way to the door and opened it just in time for me to hear the gentle strains of the *NSYNC Christmas album.

I laughed, dropping my bag as I clapped my hand over my mouth. From the ceiling hung a thousand tiny paper snowflakes and the palm tree in the corner was decked with Christmas lights, a wrapped box underneath it. It was a winter wonderland.

"Christmas is already over, though," I said, my voice wobblier than I expected.

Sam shut the door behind us. "Never for you, and I know you love the snow. So, as much as I want to see you in that bikini you bought ASAP, I thought we could make it the best of both worlds."

"I can't believe you did all this for me." I sniffled.

"Baby, I would do anything for you. Now, don't you want to open your present?"

I gave him a shaky nod and then took the red box from the floor and set it on the bed. Carefully, I removed the bow and ripped away the paper until I found all my Christmas DVDs inside.

"I thought we could have a little marathon tonight. Room service, hot bath."

I took his face in my hands and pulled him down to kiss me. "You are the perfect man. I love you."

"I love you, too, beautiful. Always have. Always will."

Sign up for the 1001 Dark Nights Newsletter
and be entered to win a Tiffany Key necklace.

There's a contest every month!

Go to www.1001DarkNights.com to subscribe.

As a bonus, all subscribers will receive a free
1001 Dark Nights story
The First Night
by Lexi Blake & M.J. Rose

Discover 1001 Dark Nights Collection Four

Go to www.1001DarkNights.com for more information.

ROCK CHICK REAWAKENING by Kristen Ashley
A Rock Chick Novella

ADORING INK by Carrie Ann Ryan
A Montgomery Ink Novella

SWEET RIVALRY by K. Bromberg

SHADE'S LADY by Joanna Wylde
A Reapers MC Novella

RAZR by Larissa Ione
A Demonica Underworld Novella

ARRANGED by Lexi Blake
A Masters and Mercenaries Novella

TANGLED by Rebecca Zanetti
A Dark Protectors Novella

HOLD ME by J. Kenner
A Stark Ever After Novella

SOMEHOW, SOME WAY by Jennifer Probst
A Billionaire Builders Novella

TOO CLOSE TO CALL by Tessa Bailey
A Romancing the Clarksons Novella

HUNTED by Elisabeth Naughton
An Eternal Guardians Novella

EYES ON YOU by Laura Kaye
A Blasphemy Novella

BLADE by Alexandra Ivy/Laura Wright
A Bayou Heat Novella

DRAGON BURN by Donna Grant
A Dark Kings Novella

TRIPPED OUT by Lorelei James
A Blacktop Cowboys® Novella

STUD FINDER by Lauren Blakely

MIDNIGHT UNLEASHED by Lara Adrian
A Midnight Breed Novella

HALLOW BE THE HAUNT by Heather Graham
A Krewe of Hunters Novella

DIRTY FILTHY FIX by Laurelin Paige
A Fixed Novella

THE BED MATE by Kendall Ryan
A Room Mate Novella

PRINCE ROMAN by CD Reiss

NO RESERVATIONS by Kristen Proby
A Fusion Novella

DAWN OF SURRENDER by Liliana Hart
A MacKenzie Family Novella

Discover 1001 Dark Nights Collection One
Go to www.1001DarkNights.com for more information.

FOREVER WICKED by Shayla Black
CRIMSON TWILIGHT by Heather Graham
CAPTURED IN SURRENDER by Liliana Hart
SILENT BITE: A SCANGUARDS WEDDING by Tina Folsom
DUNGEON GAMES by Lexi Blake
AZAGOTH by Larissa Ione
NEED YOU NOW by Lisa Renee Jones
SHOW ME, BABY by Cherise Sinclair
ROPED IN by Lorelei James
TEMPTED BY MIDNIGHT by Lara Adrian
THE FLAME by Christopher Rice
CARESS OF DARKNESS by Julie Kenner

Also from 1001 Dark Nights

TAME ME by J. Kenner

Discover 1001 Dark Nights Collection Two

Go to www.1001DarkNights.com for more information.

WICKED WOLF by Carrie Ann Ryan
WHEN IRISH EYES ARE HAUNTING by Heather Graham
EASY WITH YOU by Kristen Proby
MASTER OF FREEDOM by Cherise Sinclair
CARESS OF PLEASURE by Julie Kenner
ADORED by Lexi Blake
HADES by Larissa Ione
RAVAGED by Elisabeth Naughton
DREAM OF YOU by Jennifer L. Armentrout
STRIPPED DOWN by Lorelei James
RAGE/KILLIAN by Alexandra Ivy/Laura Wright
DRAGON KING by Donna Grant
PURE WICKED by Shayla Black
HARD AS STEEL by Laura Kaye
STROKE OF MIDNIGHT by Lara Adrian
ALL HALLOWS EVE by Heather Graham
KISS THE FLAME by Christopher Rice
DARING HER LOVE by Melissa Foster
TEASED by Rebecca Zanetti
THE PROMISE OF SURRENDER by Liliana Hart

Also from 1001 Dark Nights

THE SURRENDER GATE By Christopher Rice
SERVICING THE TARGET By Cherise Sinclair

Discover 1001 Dark Nights Collection Three

Go to www.1001DarkNights.com for more information.

HIDDEN INK by Carrie Ann Ryan
BLOOD ON THE BAYOU by Heather Graham
SEARCHING FOR MINE by Jennifer Probst
DANCE OF DESIRE by Christopher Rice
ROUGH RHYTHM by Tessa Bailey
DEVOTED by Lexi Blake
Z by Larissa Ione
FALLING UNDER YOU by Laurelin Paige
EASY FOR KEEPS by Kristen Proby
UNCHAINED by Elisabeth Naughton
HARD TO SERVE by Laura Kaye
DRAGON FEVER by Donna Grant
KAYDEN/SIMON by Alexandra Ivy/Laura Wright
STRUNG UP by Lorelei James
MIDNIGHT UNTAMED by Lara Adrian
TRICKED by Rebecca Zanetti
DIRTY WICKED by Shayla Black
THE ONLY ONE by Lauren Blakely
SWEET SURRENDER by Liliana Hart

About Kendall Ryan

A *New York Times*, *Wall Street Journal*, and *USA Today* bestselling author of more than two dozen titles, Kendall Ryan has sold over 2 million books and her books have been translated into several languages in countries around the world. Her books have also appeared on the New York Times and USA Today bestseller lists more than three dozen times. Ryan has been featured in such publications as USA Today, Newsweek, and InTouch Magazine. She lives in Texas with her husband and two sons.

Website: www.kendallryanbooks.com
Facebook: Kendall Ryan Books
Twitter: @kendallryan1

The Room Mate

By Kendall Ryan
Now Available!

This is book 1 in the Roommates series from NY Times bestseller Kendall Ryan, but each book can be read as a complete standalone as they all feature brand new couples to fall in love with.

The last time I saw my best friend's younger brother, he was a geek wearing braces. But when Cannon shows up to crash in my spare room, I get a swift reality check.

Now twenty-four, he's broad shouldered and masculine, and so sinfully sexy, I want to climb him like the jungle gyms we used to enjoy. At six-foot-something with lean muscles hiding under his T-shirt, a deep sexy voice, and full lips that pull into a smirk when he studies me, he's pure temptation.

Fresh out of a messy breakup, he doesn't want any entanglements. But I can resist, right?

I'm holding strong until the third night of our new arrangement when we get drunk and he confesses his biggest secret of all: he's cursed when it comes to sex. Apparently he's a god in bed, and women instantly fall in love with him.

I'm calling bullshit. In fact, I'm going to prove him wrong, and if I rack up a few much-needed orgasms in the process, all the better.

There's no way I'm going to fall in love with Cannon. But once we start…I realize betting against him may have been the biggest mistake of my life.

* * * *

Grabbing my shampoo and bodywash from the plastic bag, I headed across the hall for a much-needed shower. Being elbow-deep in vagina all day necessitated that, not that I minded too much. Although it wasn't a field I wanted to pursue, even I had to admit it was a pretty cool experience getting to deliver babies.

I turned on the water and stripped down while waiting for it to heat up. But when I stepped into the shower, I was hit with the mouthwatering scent of Paige's floral shampoo and bodywash. God damn . . . My cock instantly leaped to attention. I couldn't resist reaching down to grip my already rock-hard erection.

Squirting some of Paige's conditioner into my palm, I let her scent surround me as I pumped up and down in uneven pulls, the slick cream letting my fist glide over the steely flesh, each stroke bringing a wave of pleasure.

Standing under the hot spray, I thought of Paige and her luscious tits and pink cheeks as she drank in the first sight of me in five years. I wanted to do wicked things to her. Wanted to see if she'd squeak in surprise when my tongue lapped between her thighs. To find out how fast I could make her come. Would I have to work at it, learning how to pleasure her by following the sounds she made, or would she explode quickly? She did seem pretty pent up . . .

I gritted my teeth as my orgasm surged closer. Fuck, I was already about to blow. Normally I'd last much longer, but everything about this woman went straight to my cock. Moments later, my release crashed through me as I emptied into my hand, spent and breathing hard.

After rinsing off a final time, I shut off the water. With water sluicing down my body, I reached for my towel and realize I'd forgotten one. Fuck. I'd left my new towels still folded in the shopping bag. Across the hall in my room. Didn't matter. I was ninety-nine percent sure Paige was asleep in her bedroom. Grabbing my dirty clothes from the floor, I opened the bathroom door, moving with purpose toward my room—

When I ran bang into something solid. The impact knocked

the pile of clothes I'd been holding in front of my groin out of my hands.

A gray-and-brown blur flashed by my feet with a jingle of tags. Paige gasped in surprise and stumbled a step back. Instinctively, I reached out to steady her, gripping her shoulders.

"I'm sorry," I murmured, noticing that she slept in nothing but a T-shirt that barely covered her ass. The thin material hugged her curves and left her delicious rack on display.

After she righted herself, Paige's gaze wandered down the length of my nude torso, stopping at my crotch. Her eyes widened and her full lips parted, the apples of her cheeks turning a pretty shade of pink. My erection hadn't fully died yet; my spent cock still hung long and heavy between my thighs. And under her heated gaze, it twitched with interest, thickening and beginning to rise again.

"You can touch it if you want," I murmured, amused by her response. There had been more than just astonishment in those wide, pretty eyes. I was pretty sure there was interest, and maybe even desire.

A noise of strangled surprise escaped her lips.

This was just too much fun. I wasn't in a hurry to go anywhere, but I cleared my throat and her gaze jumped back up to mine.

"You okay?" I asked.

"Enchilada had to pee," she murmured, breathless.

Right, the dog. So that was what had run past us into Paige's bedroom. I nodded once, a smirk pulling up my mouth. I'd have to sneak the little mop a few thank-you treats in the morning. This was the most fun I'd had all day.

"Good night," she squeaked, then darted around me into her bedroom, where she promptly slammed the door. I could imagine her behind it, her legs sagging as she braced herself on the wall, her chest heaving as she tried to recover.

On behalf of 1001 Dark Nights,

Liz Berry and M.J. Rose would like to thank ~

Steve Berry
Doug Scofield
Kim Guidroz
Jillian Stein
InkSlinger PR
Dan Slater
Asha Hossain
Chris Graham
Fedora Chen
Kasi Alexander
Jessica Johns
Dylan Stockton
Richard Blake
BookTrib After Dark
and Simon Lipskar